Y0-BPV-290

Just in Time

Legacy Series, Book 5

PAULA KAY

Copyright © 2015 Paula Kay

All rights reserved.

ISBN: 0692473300
ISBN-13: 978-0692473306

DEDICATION

To Louise.
Thank you for your friendship, love and support.

TABLE OF CONTENTS

CHAPTER 1

Jemma Foster woke up to the annoying sound of her phone ringing *and* a splitting headache. God, how much had she had to drink last night anyway? It was all a bit of a blur—as were most of the evenings that she'd been spending with Dex lately—but she vaguely remembered coming in around two, careful not to wake Chase and somewhat surprised that he hadn't been waiting up for her—what with her mom being out of town and all.

She finally reached for her phone, noticing that it was eleven o'clock and that the call was from her mother. She debating ignoring it to go back to sleep, but she needed to get up to use the bathroom anyway.

"Hello."

Her voice was low and horrid-sounding, even to her own ear.

"Are you just waking up? Geez, Jemma, it's eleven o'clock."

"Yeah, well, it's also Saturday."

She was still annoyed at her mom because of the argument they'd had about Jemma not going to New York with her. It was some big fashion show, but Jemma had had a party that she didn't want to miss. She used to enjoy traveling with her mom, grandma, and Kylie, but lately it seemed like all she and her mom did was fight about what Jemma could and couldn't do.

She heard her mom sigh on the other end of the phone. "Well, I've been trying to reach you all morning. Can you please do me a favor and find a paper in the office for me?"

Now it was Jemma's turn to sigh. "Yeah, okay. Just give me a minute to use the bathroom."

She was quick about it, by this time wanting to get off the phone with her mom to get a cup of coffee.

She grabbed the phone off the bed as she made her way downstairs to the office.

"Okay, I'm in your office."

She walked over to the window to raise the blind, noticing what a gorgeous day it was outside. Maybe she really did take where they lived for granted—that was what her mom and Chase were always telling her. She did love San Diego, and she knew that she was lucky to have spent most of her youth in the massive La Jolla beach home that her mom's best friend had left her—that Arianna had left the both of them when she'd passed away.

She turned her attention back to her mom on the

other end of the phone.

"Okay, so go over to the gray file cabinet in the corner—the one next to the bookshelf."

Blu gave Jemma the rest of the instructions that enabled her to read the information off the particular paperwork that she needed.

"Thanks, kiddo."

"Mom. Stop. I hate when you call me that."

"Well, I hate it that you're mad at me all of the time."

Jemma felt a slight pang of something but it didn't last long.

"I'm not mad at you all the time—just some of the time—when you're being a pain."

"You mean when I'm not so quick to give you what you want."

"Anyway, I gotta go."

"What are you going to do today?"

"I dunno. I might go to the beach, I guess."

"With who?"

"Mom, please. I don't know."

Her mom hated her boyfriend and pretty much had forbidden Jemma from seeing Dex. There was no way his name was even coming up in this conversation right now.

"Jemma, it's normal for a mom to want to know what her seventeen-year-old kid is doing while they're away."

"Well, Chase is here."

Jemma did like her mom's husband—and well, after being in her life for so many years he was her father, really. But he'd definitely been taking her mom's side lately. They were just both always on her case about something.

"Jemma. I know Chase is working today. You need to be sure to text him, please, to let him know what you're doing."

"Yeah, okay, Mom. I will. Now I gotta go."

"Why don't you call Claire to do something?"

Claire used to be Jemma's best friend, but they hadn't even talked for at least the past six months—not since Jemma had started hanging out with Dex and—well, Claire had her friends that Jemma didn't really like any more than Claire had liked Jemma's new boyfriend.

"Mom, how many times do I have to tell you? Claire and I really aren't good friends any more."

Her mom sighed on the other end of the line. Jemma was sure that she and Claire's mom had probably been talking about how the pair of them hadn't had much to do with one another lately. It used to be nice that their moms were also best friends; now Jemma just found it completely annoying.

"Mom, I gotta go—"

"Okay, wait—"

"—Mom." Jemma was getting seriously irritated.

"Kylie wants to talk to you."

Jemma relaxed for second and walked over to the chaise lounge in the office.

"Hi, Jemma."

Jemma smiled as soon as she heard her sister's voice on the other end of the line. Kylie was seven and one of the few people whom Jemma adored these days.

"Hi, Ky. Are you having fun in New York?"

"Yeah, Grandma took me to the big toy store yesterday—you know, that one with the giant keyboard you can step on."

Jemma smiled. "FAO Schwarz?"

"Yeah, that's the one. Anyway, I got you something and it's a surprise so don't ask me to tell you, okay?"

Jemma laughed. "Okay, I won't. You do realize that I'm getting a bit old for toys, don't you?"

"Well, Grandma said that you would like this one. Well, it's not really a toy. It's kinda like a project that Grandma and I are gonna do together."

"Ky? Are you trying to give me some hints?" God, this kid did crack her up sometimes.

"No, I'm not. I'm not saying one other word about it."

Jemma imagine Kylie crossing her slight arms in front of her, her lovely blond curls springing as she shook her head.

"Okay, then. Listen, I gotta get going."

"Okay. Jemma?"

"Yeah?"

"I miss you. I wish you came with us. I always have more fun when you're here too."

Jemma smiled, realizing that her complete irritation of

the morning had melted away.

"I know. I miss you too. But you have fun and get all of your homework done with Grandma so that we can do something when you come home tomorrow, okay?"

"Okay. I love you, Jemma."

"I love you too. Bye."

She crossed the room to kneel down to shut the file cabinet door that she'd left open, and then something caught her eye. She reached under the small space of the bookshelf she was kneeling next to and pulled out a thin metal box. The box was locked, and immediately Jemma wanted to know what was inside.

She wasn't really one to snoop through her mom's things, but then again she really felt like her mom hadn't been giving her the most privacy lately either. And besides, how could she resist? What could possibly be inside?

She didn't really think her mom was all that interesting, even though she knew that Blu Foster's "black-n-blu" clothing line had become very famous in the world of fashion. All of Jemma's friends had always thought that she'd had the coolest mom of them all, and Jemma definitely always had the nicest clothing. That was one thing she could really appreciate about her mom even though these days Jemma didn't care too much about her clothes. She was quite happy to wear her ripped jean shorts, T-shirts, and sneakers, which she knew drove her mom slightly crazy at times.

Jemma was trying to think of any place where her mom might have put the key for the metal box she was holding in her hand. She checked the obvious drawers in her mom's desk. A glance back in the file cabinet didn't seem to turn anything up. Something from her memory—probably something she'd seen in a movie once—caused her to swipe her hand underneath first the shelf of the bookshelf, then the underside of her mom's desk. Bingo. Her fingers moved over something taped underneath the desk.

Her morning had possibly just gotten a bit more interesting.

CHAPTER 2

Jemma sat on the floor of her mom's office looking at the thin envelope that had held the birth certificate which was now lying beside her on the floor. She didn't know whether to scream or cry. Quite possibly she was in shock. Quite possibly everything in her world had just completely shifted and she was about to go insane.

When she saw the name on the envelope—Jessica—she knew. It didn't take a lot to put two and two together once she looked over the paper inside. Her grandma had slipped up a few times. Her mind now grabbed for those memories—going back to the earliest days that her grandmother had moved in with them. Jemma had been nine at the time, and she was almost sure that she could remember her grandma calling her Jessica on a few occasions.

She was the Jessica White on the birth certificate.

Her heart was pounding wildly in her chest as she grabbed up the paper and ran to her room, the tears starting to come, fast and furious. She rummaged in her purse for her cigarettes. God, she really needed one. Had she smoked through a whole pack last night? Her coat pocket. She remembered Dex zipping them in right before they'd gotten on his motorcycle to come home. If she was lucky, he may have even slipped a little surprise in there for her.

She hadn't really done anything too bad in terms of drugs—not like what Dex and his friends did anyway. She didn't have the nerve to try coke or Ecstasy, no matter how many times Dex had asked her to do it with him. But lately she had finally given in when it came to smoking a little pot—and what she wouldn't give for a little hit right about now. Who could blame her after the shock that she'd just received?

She needed to breathe. She stepped outside onto the big deck off her room, the sun hitting her in the eyes, reminding her of the headache that somehow had been long forgotten in just the last twenty minutes or so. She pulled on the sunglasses that she also found in her coat pocket and peered into the half-empty pack of cigarettes. No such luck on the weed. She eyed the phone that she'd placed next to her on the small table. She'd call Dex in a minute—see if he'd come pick her up, give her a little something else to calm her nerves. Right now she just needed to think.

Even in her shock she had to laugh at herself. Her mom was always talking about how cool-headed she'd always been, even as a little girl—able to keep her wits about her no matter what was happening around her, her mom had always said.

Her mother. What the hell?

Jemma lit one of the cigarettes, inhaling a deep puff as she looked at the piece of paper on her lap. Jessica Lynne White. It was a different birth date but the same month and year. And the only parent listed was the mother, as Linda White.

Her grandmother. Only it wasn't her grandmother at all.

Jemma shocked herself at the sobs that were suddenly coming out of her. What was happening right now? What did this all mean? Had her whole life been a lie? Her name, her birth date, her mother? Who had she been calling her mother all these years?

She screamed as her mother's face flashed in her head—a lifetime of memories from before they lived at the beach. She and her mother in San Francisco staying up late to watch movies and eat popcorn, long drives in the car when her mom had a day off—and all of the memories that came after their lives had changed so much. After Arianna had passed away, after they moved and started having a better life. The trips to Italy to see Lia and Antonio, the trips to Guatemala to visit Gigi and Douglas. God, did they all know about her? Did anyone else know that her mom was really her sister.

Blu Foster—or whatever her real name was—was really Jemma's sister.

The idea was almost absurd, but even in her shocked

state, Jemma was putting the pieces together, remembering how it had been when her grandmother had first come to San Diego to see them. Her mother had tried to keep them apart and over the years, Jemma had asked enough questions and gotten enough answers to put together the missing pieces about why her grandmother had not been in their lives before then—Linda had been upfront with Jemma about her past once Jemma had gotten older and started asking questions. She had always appreciated that about her grandmother. But now? Now she didn't know what to think.

She wiped angrily at the tears that were falling again as she let herself think about the lie that she'd been living. Had they ever planned to tell her the truth? She was months away from her eighteenth birthday. Was it possible that they were going to tell her then? She shook her head, knowing the truth deep inside her. No. They had never planned on telling her. No one had, or they would have done so before now.

She swallowed her sobs down as she reached for her phone to text Dex. She definitely needed something more than a cigarette.

Where r u? Can u come get me at the house? Bring supplies.

She watched her phone for a few minutes, willing him to respond but knowing he was probably in bed sleeping off last night's binge. She knew he probably stayed up partying long after he'd dropped her off at two. He rarely went to sleep before five o'clock in the morning, something that drove Jemma crazy because he was never up for doing anything with her during the daytime.

She took a long drag from her cigarette, reminding herself to get rid of all the evidence afterwards, as the last time her mom caught her smoking she completely flipped out. Jemma laughed even as she was having the thought. It was crazy. Did she even have a reason to care what her so-called mother thought any more—who even had the right to tell her anything that she should or shouldn't be doing?

She didn't know whether to laugh or cry. All she knew was that she wanted to get loaded, and now she had to just wait for her good-for-nothing boyfriend to wake the heck up and come to her during her time of need. Laughable. If only she were a comedian, this would be some good material she had going just now. Was there seriously anyone she could talk to—anyone who would understand?

Gigi.

Jemma knew better than to think that she didn't have anyone in her life who cared about her. She had Gigi and Douglas—Lia and Antonio too, but Gigi really had been like a grandmother to Jemma, and Jemma loved her more than almost anyone. She trusted Gigi more than anyone, that was for sure. She picked up her phone to send her a quick message, instantly feeling annoyed with herself as she saw that she'd not responded to Gigi's last text to her, sent a few days ago.

Hey, pretty girl. I miss you. When can we talk?

Jemma sent a text back.

Sorry, Gi, that I didn't get back to you sooner. Everyone is OK but something bad has happened.

She waited a few seconds and then added, *I could really use someone to talk to right now if you're available?*

She looked at the time, realizing that Gigi was probably right in the middle of lunch with the kids at the orphanage. She finished her cigarette and settled back into her favorite chair on the deck. She used to love to sit and draw out here. She couldn't even remember the last time that she'd done so. It seemed like ever since Dex had come into her life, a lot of her old hobbies had gotten less interesting to her. But even as she had the thought she knew it wasn't true. She would always love to draw and paint. She was an artist, just like her mother—that's what her mom always said anyway. Jemma shook her head as if doing so could tame her jumbled thoughts about her mother—about Blu.

She pulled out the old sketchpad from the drawer of the table next to her—right where she'd left it all those months ago. She smiled as she leafed through the sketches one by one. The earliest ones were those that she'd done at the orphanage—the summer she was fifteen. She remembered that her mom and Chase had given the nice sketchpad to her as part of a care package that they'd sent her while she was away for the summer.

She smiled at the memory. She had fought the idea of

going to Guatemala to stay with Gigi when they'd all discussed it, but her mom, grandma, and Chase thought it would be good for her and—well, she didn't really have a choice in the matter. In the end, though, it had been one of the best summers that she could remember. She'd made friends there—much different than her friends in La Jolla—and she liked that about the place. She learned early on that she could be herself there, and she remembered a certain kind of freedom that she felt swimming in the river and helping with the younger kids.

She came to a picture that she'd sketched of Gigi. The memory of it made her laugh. She'd been so patient with her and so sure that Jemma could get it just right. Every day she'd sit still for at least ten minutes at a time, her legs dangling off the dock, sometimes a child in her lap or by her side. Always smiling, always saying the same thing to Jemma. "An artist must sketch, my dear. And you are an artist," she'd say, making Jemma laugh every time.

It had been a great summer, and that was when she and Gigi had grown very close. Thinking back, Jemma supposed Gigi had known just what she needed. It was that rough time—the time when kids really don't like to share things with their mothers—well, that hadn't really changed for Jemma, not yet, anyway—and now? Well, now her life was just a big mess; forget sharing anything with her mother.

The ding of her phone interrupted her thoughts. *Gigi.*

PAULA KAY

CHAPTER 3

Jemma's incoming text was from Dex, not Gigi.

Can't come yet 2 hungover.

Reading it only made Jemma feel more annoyed.

Seriously? Please. Something bad has happened. I kinda need you.

She'd give him five minutes to respond—and then what? She wasn't sure, but she knew she had to get out of here. She had to figure out what she was going to do. She was kind of surprised that she hadn't gone off on her mom yet. But it felt weird doing it over the phone. She needed to be able to see her mom's face when she told her that she knew the truth. She needed to be able to see them both—her mom and her grandma. So that would wait until tomorrow. She just wanted to get through the rest of the day—hopefully her so-called boyfriend could help her with that.

She glanced down at her phone again to see another incoming text.

Okay babe. Be there soon.

She took a deep breath as she responded. At least he

wasn't gonna totally leave her hanging. She'd give him the benefit of the doubt for now—as long as he actually showed up. She couldn't help thinking it, as he'd flaked on her in the past on more than one occasion.

Deep down she knew that her mom and Chase could be right about Dex. She wasn't exactly sure what she did see in him, but she knew that he was exciting in a way that she seemed to need right now. She loved being on the back of his motorcycle with him—if her mom knew that she was still riding with him, she'd have a fit.

One time they'd caught them just as Dex was dropping her off and her mom and Chase had come home early from something. Chase had had words with Dex right in the driveway and Jemma had been beyond embarrassed.

It really hadn't fazed Dex all that much. Jemma suspected he was used to the "bad boy" reputation when it came to parents, and he didn't seem to mind. After that had happened, her mom had forbidden her to see him, which only made Jemma start sneaking around. And Dex was more than happy to oblige. He seemed to enjoy showing her a world of drinking and drugs—a way of life that he'd been living for quite some time. He wasn't any older than she was—yet to turn eighteen himself—but he and his older brother, Slade, had lived on their own since Dex was sixteen.

Jemma had the wits about her to know that she was playing with fire in a way, but she wasn't really doing anything that other kids her age weren't doing too—and as long as she stayed away from the harder stuff, she figured she'd be fine. But the truth was—today, anyway—she was almost tempted. It wouldn't take much convincing from Dex for her to try one of those sweet drugs that he was always promising would take all of her concerns away.

In the past when he'd said such things, she'd almost laughed because she could hear her mother's voice in her head. What concerns did she really have anyway? Not many, if you were asking her mom and Chase, but today everything had changed. Today was the day that she'd found out that her whole life had been a lie.

Jemma grabbed her things, heading back into her room to get dressed. She really needed that coffee and at least a bite to eat before Dex showed up. She brushed her straight blond hair back into a ponytail, washed her face, and brushed her teeth. She studied herself in the mirror for a minute. Her mother always told her that she was beautiful but she didn't really see it herself. Well, maybe she was what one would call a "girl next door" kind of pretty, but she didn't have the beauty of a model, or anything that would cause someone to look twice at her. That was how she felt about her looks anyway.

She heard Dex's motorcycle coming up the driveway just as she was sipping the last of her coffee. Chase had left a note for her in the kitchen, saying that he'd be back before dinner and asking her to text him with her plans. He also had said that he'd appreciate it if she would join him for dinner if she didn't have anything else going on. Normally Jemma wouldn't mind the chance to hang out with Chase, but she honestly didn't know if she could do it without spilling the beans about what she'd learned today. Somehow it didn't feel right that he should know before her mother—although even as she had the thought, she wondered if she should even care. Or why did she even care?

She sighed as she grabbed her purse and jacket to run out the door before Dex starting honking for a second time. She didn't really need for him to give her nosy neighbors anything to talk about.

She smiled as she got near him. Dex definitely did have that "bad boy" look about him, something she hadn't really realized that she was attracted to until they'd met at a beach party six months ago. It was his tattoo that had first captured her attention—a giant snake-like creature curving around his bicep—the perfect excuse for conversation, and she'd been slightly tipsy that day that she'd approached him.

She leaned up to give him a quick kiss on the lips, while he took his helmet off to hand to her.

"Hey, babe."

"Hey, yourself. Thanks for coming to get me."

"Yeah, well, I wasn't exactly feeling so hot this morning. I'm still not, really. But whatever. What's going on with you and what's with the urgency?"

Jemma thought he seemed more annoyed than concerned, but she tried to brush it off.

"Can we go somewhere? Our spot down at the beach?"

He was nodding his head and tapping the pocket of his shirt. "Yep. Can do."

Good, he brought something to smoke. She was happy about that. She didn't smoke it all the time like he did, but whenever she did, she noticed that it made her feel relaxed, and today her nerves felt about as tight as they could be. She needed to relax like never before, and she was counting on Dex to help her with that. Now, counting on him to be a good listening ear for this new problem that had come up for her? That would remain to be seen. Her hopes weren't as high with that one.

"So spill it. What's up with you?" Dex handed her his joint and watched her intently as she took her first puff, leaning back against the big piece of driftwood that they'd found to shelter them from watchful eyes further down the beach.

It was a secluded spot she'd discovered one day while out for a long run. There were a lot of big rocks and some brush separating the area from the more popular beach, so most people turned around by the time they made it to this spot along the sandy coast. She and Dex had starting coming here when they wanted to be alone to smoke, have a drink, or talk. Well, they rarely did much talking really—more like a good make-out session.

She studied his face for a full minute before she answered him.

"I found something today—in my mom's office."

"Yeah, what was it? Something kinky that you didn't want to know about?" He laughed and she punched him in the arm.

"No, nothing like that. Something that has to do with me."

"Well, what was it? You seem pretty freaked out—or at least more freaked out than I've seen you in the past." He leaned over to give her a quick kiss on the nose, a move she guessed that was meant to keep her from punching him again.

"I found my birth certificate."

"Okay. And?"

"And pretty much everything I believed my whole life is a lie." Saying it out loud was causing the tears to come again. She hated it—what she'd found out. That her mom was a liar. Even when she was the most angry at her mom, she always felt that she was on her side. But now—now she really couldn't believe that she'd been keeping the truth from her all these years.

"Okay. I think you're going to have to spell this out for me, because I'm not quite getting what you're saying. Is this about your father?"

She had told Dex on one occasion that she didn't

really know anything about her father—that it was a closed subject between her mother and her—one that Jemma just didn't care to bring up anymore.

"Well?"

God, how was it that she hadn't even stopped to think about her father? She knew it was that man she'd seen so many years ago—the man that her mom had been so disgusted by. The thought turned her stomach because she remembered feeling frightened of him then, sitting in the car watching him yell at her grandmother.

"Well, what?"

"Well, as it turns out my mom is really my sister and my grandmother who lives with us is really my mother." It seemed so absurd coming out of her mouth that she didn't know whether to start laughing or crying again.

The look on Dex's face made her burst into tears, burying her head into his chest as he held her to him.

"God, Jem. That *is* some heavy stuff."

She pulled her head away long enough to look him in the eyes. "I know. Crazy, huh? I feel like I'm losing my mind—like none of this is real and I'm going to wake up from a nightmare any second."

"Have you talked to her? To your mom—or what are you even going to call her now?"

"I don't know. I guess I'm still calling her Mom. I mean—well, she's the only mom I've ever known." Jemma stood up as the tears started again. "What can she possibly say to make it better? What can either of them say? And they're out of town until tomorrow, so she doesn't even know that I found out."

"Babe. That really stinks. I mean, I thought your family life was so much better than mine, but at least I've known all along that most of my family were jerks. Yours have only been pretending not to be, apparently."

She smiled just a little, appreciating the fact that he seemed to want to lighten the mood. He wasn't used to seeing her so intense. She'd not really bothered to show him anything other than "party girl Jemma" up until this point.

"So do you have anything else in that jacket of yours?" She grinned at him, ready to be done talking—ready to be done thinking for now. She really just wanted to get wasted and forget for a few hours that any of it had even happened.

Dex pulled a small flask from his inside coat pocket and handed it to her as she giggled at him.

"You're so old school with your fancy silver flask and all." She took the lid off and drank a big swig of the vodka, anticipating the nice burn in her throat that was coming.

"Yeah, well, it's good enough for you, isn't it?" He took it from her to take a swig himself, then pulled her to him, the length of her body fitting up snug against his tall frame. He kissed her hard on the lips and she didn't resist. "Should we go back to my place? I think Slade is gone for the day."

So far Jemma and Dex's brother hadn't really hit it off so well. They seemed to regard one another with equal amounts of skepticism. Dex had told her that Slade couldn't understand what a pretty little rich girl was doing with the likes of him—slumming it on their side of the tracks, he'd called it. Ever since then, Jemma only felt weird when she was around him, so she tried to stay away from their apartment as much as possible.

Dex was waiting for her to answer him. She bit the inside of her lip thinking about what to say, because she didn't want to make him angry after he'd come over to help make her feel better.

"Do you mind if we just stay here for awhile? I don't feel like being inside today. The fresh air is helping to clear my mind, I think." She leaned over to give him a quick kiss on the cheek, hoping it would appease him, but knowing that it probably wouldn't—not for long anyway. She could tell that he was tired and he'd need more sleep to be ready to party again tonight—an endless cycle around his place, one that she was usually only able to handle on the weekends.

"Whatever you say, babe. But I'm not gonna stay for too long, okay?"

"Sure. Just a little while. Maybe for one more of those magic smokes I'm sure you still have?" She laughed and he grinned back at her, happy to oblige as he pulled the joint out of his pocket.

Yes, she'd just sit here with Dex for a little while

longer. Everything was going to be okay. She'd worry about everything later. She laid her head back against Dex's chest and closed her eyes, barely noticing the tears that were still there, sneaking out from beneath her closed eyelids.

CHAPTER 4

Jemma walked in the door, anxious to get in touch with Gigi. She'd gotten a text from her while she was with Dex saying to message her as soon as she could. Dex had been surprisingly more sympathetic than Jemma would have imagined he'd be, but Gigi was really the person that Jemma wanted to talk to. She couldn't help but have the feeling that Dex was secretly—or most of the time not so secretly—wanting her to rebel against her family the way that he'd done with his own. He'd had his own freedom for a while now and didn't really get why Jemma wouldn't want that also.

Jemma did want that. More than anything now. She'd been counting the days until her eighteenth birthday next month. And she was luckier than most her age in that she'd always known about the trust—the money that Arianna had left her. She'd finally get it when she turned eighteen, and lately she and her mom had had more than a few conversations—or more like arguments—about it.

Her mom said that Arianna had left the money to

Jemma to be able to pursue her goals—an education, travel, her dance—whatever Jemma's passions were. Jemma had to smile whenever she thought about the dancing. She did have memories of putting on little shows for Arianna with her tutu on. She knew that Arianna had provided that early education for her and she remembered loving it at one time, but she'd given up dance long ago.

Jemma sighed. She really didn't know what she was passionate about these days. She'd thought about going to college at one time—or art school—but now? Now she just wanted to get away from her family—well, from her mom and grandma. But not Kylie. She couldn't imagine not having her sister in her life.

Jemma sent Gigi a text as she was going up the stairs to her room.

Hi, Gi. Sorry I didn't get back to you earlier. I'm home now. Can you talk?

Just as soon as she'd flopped across her bed, her phone rang. She answered, immediately bursting into tears.

"Jemma? Honey, are you there?"

Hearing Gigi's voice on the other end of the phone was what Jemma had needed all day—ever since she'd found the metal box.

"Jemma? You're scaring me a little bit."

"I-I'm here. Sorry." Jemma tried to take a deep breath to stop her tears.

"Honey, what's wrong? Is everyone okay?"

"Yes. No. I mean, no one is hurt but, Gi, I found something out—something about my mom and me."

Gigi was silent for several seconds on the other end of the line. Jemma had already guessed that it was possible that there were other people in her life who knew the truth—if anyone did, it would be Gigi and Lia—and Chase, of course. But she wouldn't blame them. It wasn't for them to tell. She wasn't naive enough to think otherwise, even though it hurt her deeply.

"What happened, Jemma?"

She could hear Gigi's sigh and imagined her sitting back on the small sofa in her little home at the orphanage.

Jemma was crying again. She couldn't help it, and it was odd because she hadn't cried in ages—not tears that had to do with anything other than anger. She tried to get herself together enough to speak.

"I was in Mom's office this morning—she needed me to get something for her. And I found it."

"What? What did you find?"

"My birth certificate." And there was no holding back the tears again.

Gigi waited for a few seconds while Jemma cried on the other end of the phone.

"Sweetie. It's going to be okay."

Her voice was calm but her words were irritating to Jemma. No, it wasn't going to be okay. How could anything ever be okay with this situation? Nothing between her and her mother—or her grandmother, for that matter—was ever going to be the same again, and it most certainly was not going to be okay.

"It's not okay, Gi." Jemma shouted the words into the phone, and she heard Gigi's deep intake of breath as she prepared to speak.

"Honey, have you spoken to your—to your mom?"

Jemma was calming down just a bit, trying to collect her thoughts.

"No. She's out of town until tomorrow."

"And your grandma?"

"She's with her. They don't know anything yet. I-I thought it would be better to wait until they got home, but honestly, Gi…" Jemma's voice trailed off as the tears came again. "I don't even really care. I don't want to be here."

"Honey, everything's going to be okay. I know it's a shock right now but maybe once you talk to your mom—to your grandma—everything will make more sense. No one was ever trying to hurt you. You do know that, right?"

It sounded like Gigi had covered the phone for a second, and Jemma guessed that Douglas was in the room.

"Jemma, Douglas would like to speak with you, okay?"

"Okay."

Jemma had great respect for Douglas and she'd really

grown close with him over the years. He'd been the only person in her life to fulfill the role of a grandfather, and it had suited them both perfectly. She trusted Douglas and she knew that her mother had always felt the same about him. If anyone knew the whole story about how this had all happened, it would be Douglas. Her mother would have kept it to herself for as long as she could have. Jemma knew that about her mom. But if and when she'd needed to tell someone, Jemma was pretty sure that he would have been her confidant.

"Jemma?"

"Yeah."

"I'm sure that you're feeling pretty confused about everything right now. I don't know the whole story—about what you found, I mean—but I can imagine that you're really wanting some answers."

"Yeah, like how the heck is it that my whole life has been a lie!" She shouted the words into the phone and she felt the anger taking over once again—it was a more comfortable feeling for her, something she understood more than the tears.

"Honey, I can only imagine how shocked you must be—and of course you need to talk to your mother—to your grandmother—but I can tell you that it's not true that your life has been a lie. I know how much love that there is—and I think you know that too."

Jemma was quiet on her end of the phone.

"There were reasons why your mom—why she did

what she did. Only she can explain those to you, and I do know that the decision to keep this from you wasn't made lightly. She never wanted to hurt you—neither of them did. Jemma, you know that they've only always wanted the best for you—that's all any of us have ever wanted."

"I know."

Jemma did know that. No matter what had happened over the years—and there had been a lot of changes— she'd always had the strong sense of family and support, not just from her mom and Chase, but the others too. They all loved her. She did know that deep down, but right now—in the moment—she really didn't care about any of that.

"I'm gonna put Gigi back on the phone. Jemma?"

"Yeah?"

"Do you want me to call your mom? To talk to her first?"

"No. Please don't do that."

I want to be the one—to see the shock and the look of fear on my mom's face. It was the fierceness of the teenage rebel she'd been trying to become the past few months— caught up in that space between wanting her independence more than anything and trying to coexist with her family and the rules that she'd been made to follow.

"Okay. I won't. Here's Gigi now. We love you. Everything's going to be okay."

"Honey?"

It was Gigi's voice again on the other end, and Jemma could picture her now, sitting in that small but lovely little hut in the middle of the jungle in Guatemala. Jemma almost caught herself smiling as she thought about it.

"Yeah, I'm here."

"I—I want to be sure—I just have to say—"

Gigi was struggling to get the words out and Jemma wondered what exactly she was thinking.

"I want to be sure that you aren't going to do anything—anything that you'd regret."

Jemma smiled despite the seriousness of the conversation. She wouldn't hurt herself—not intentionally anyway. She was angry and kind of impulsive these days, but she wasn't totally stupid. Well, she wasn't so much depressed as she was angry. That was the bottom line.

"That depends on what exactly you're talking about. If you're asking me if I'm gonna off myself—no, honestly, that thought hasn't entered my mind. If you're asking me if I'm gonna go off on my mother when she gets home—yes, I'm sure there are going to be some harsh words, and I won't be thinking about what I'll be regretting at that time."

Jemma let herself relax for a minute, knowing that she needed to cool it with Gigi, who was obviously worried about her.

"Gi, no. I'm not going to hurt myself—or anyone, if that's what you're thinking."

"I know you wouldn't. I mean deep down I know that, but honestly it's been so long since we've really talked, and I know that you've been going through some changes—and some hard times lately."

Jemma was starting to get the bigger picture of what Gigi was referring to. No doubt, her mom had already talked to her about Dex and some of the so-called issues they'd been having with her lately.

"I assume that you're referring to my boyfriend that Mom hates."

"Well, she did mention that you'd been hanging out with a different crowd of people lately. And I know it's not easy, being your age—what with peer pressure and all—"

"You don't have to worry about me when it comes to peer pressure," Jemma cut her off. "I do the things I do because I want to do them, not because Dex or anyone is making me."

Her words sounded harsher than what she meant them, at least in terms of what she'd ever say to Gigi.

"I know you're a strong girl, Jemma. You always have been. And a smart girl. Don't forget that."

Jemma smiled, despite still feeling slightly irritated.

"Thank you for calling me. I do appreciate it, you know."

"I know, honey. I'm always here for you. You know that. Douglas and I love you very much."

Jemma felt tears stinging her eyes. She didn't know

when she'd been this emotional.

"Thank you. And I love you both too. Even when I'm being a brat." She laughed, trying to lighten the mood.

"You're not a brat. Well, not most of the time. Promise me that we'll talk again soon and you'll let me know how everything goes?"

"Yeah, I promise. Bye."

Jemma clicked off the phone and sank down into her bed. She needed a good nap. She toyed with the idea of checking out the liquor cabinet downstairs but she didn't have the energy to do anything other than close her eyes—no matter how badly she wanted to forget her problems.

CHAPTER 5

Jemma woke up feeling very disoriented as she reached for her phone to check the time, surprised to see that it was already seven-thirty. She also saw that she had several missed calls and texts from Chase. Darn it. She'd forgotten to send him a note. She opened up his last text, sent about an hour earlier.

Sorry. Ended up working a late party tonight. Text me back and let me know what you are doing and that you are okay. Please, Jemma.

She felt slightly guilty reading Chase's note. He was a good guy and she'd liked him from the moment she and her mom first met him, so many years ago when she'd been even younger than Kylie was now. Even after all her mom's fame and success as a designer, Chase continued to work pretty long hours as a chef—just because he loved it so much. Jemma had recently asked him about it when they were discussing her own future plans about college or whatever else she thought that she might like to do. She'd asked Chase why he continued to work and he'd talked to her about the passion behind his cooking—

43

that yes, he did enjoy cooking for his family, but there was something about the feeling that came along with knowing that your paying clients were so satisfied by the expertise that they'd paid for. Then he just laughed and said that mostly he never liked school—food was more his thing growing up. He was lucky that his parents had supported him in choosing it over college.

Jemma sent him a quick note back before she had time to forget about him again.

Sorry, C. Meant to call you earlier, but fell asleep. Going to the movies with a friend tonight. Be home late.

A quick second later, her phone buzzed with a reply.

Be good. Be careful and be home by 1.

Okay. Whatever. And she had no intention of being home early tonight. She needed a night out. She deserved a night out after the day she'd had.

Will do. See ya.

She sent the text and then brought up Dex's number. When he dropped her off earlier, he'd said that he would come back to pick her up if it wasn't too late by the time she was ready.

She was really tired of having to depend on him for rides all the time. She'd had a sweet ride in the new BMW that her mom had gotten for her when she'd turned sixteen, but when Chase found her parking in the driveway one night after drinking, both he and her mom had gone ballistic on her. They took her car away with no talk of if or when she could have it back. She didn't blame them really. She knew it was stupid to drive drunk, and she usually didn't press her luck too much with it. Chase had caught her after a particularly crazy night and now she was paying for it by having to bum rides all the time.

She waited for Dex to answer his phone, hoping that he was actually awake by this time.

"Hello...Dex's answering service, how can I assist you?"

Jemma didn't recognize the girl's voice on the other line, but she sounded drunk—and stupid.

"Can I talk to Dex?" Jemma rolled her eyes for no one's benefit but her own. She had fun with Dex and his crew over at the apartment but sometimes—always if she was around them when she was sober—the whole bunch of them got on her nerves. All they did was party, and it did get a bit old at times.

"Hey, babe. Are you ready to come over?"

"Who was the girl that answered your phone? And are you okay to come get me?"

"You mean as in am I drunk yet? The answer to that is no. Not quite enough yet, because I was waiting for you, my darling."

Jemma laughed. "And the girl?"

"Oh, that's Andrea, Slade's friend who is down from LA."

"And your friend too, Dexter."

Jemma could hear the girl's voice right up next to the phone and wondered for a second if she should feel jealous. More than anything, she just found her already annoying by the sound of her voice, and she hoped that the night wouldn't be totally unbearable.

"Yeah, right." She laughed, deciding to just brush it off. "Are you coming to get me, then? I should probably leave before it gets too late. I don't wanna risk Chase getting home first."

"No. That would not be good."

She was sure that Dex was thinking about the last run-in he'd had with Chase in the driveway. It wasn't anything that either of them wanted to repeat.

"Okay, babe. I'll come get you now."

"Thanks. See you in a few."

Jemma hung up the phone and went to put on some jeans and a touch of make-up. She usually didn't bother too much with how she looked around Dex and his friends, but for some reason tonight she felt like she wanted to pretty herself up a little bit. Maybe it was the sound of that stupid girl's voice that was getting to her after all.

The party at Dex's was in full swing by the time Jemma got there. She'd picked Andrea out of the crowd instantly, and for half an hour the girl hadn't left her side, deciding that they'd be instant best friends—and once Jemma had gotten a few drinks in her, she was happy to oblige. She hadn't been hanging out with many of her girlfriends for a long time, so the female company was something she welcomed even though she hadn't even really been thinking about it.

She didn't mean to, but she made an instant assessment of Andrea. She could tell she was on something—heavier than pot for sure, and Jemma was pretty certain that she caught a glimpse of some marks on Andrea's arms underneath her sleeves. She told Jemma that she was twenty-two, the same age as Slade—that they'd met the week before at a raging party in LA. Then she disappeared into one of the back bedrooms and Jemma didn't see her again for most of the night.

Jemma sat back against the worn sofa, drinking her vodka and smoking a cigarette. She was pretty sure that this was exactly the type of scenario that had been playing in Gigi's mind when they'd spoken earlier. Jemma kept telling herself that the lifestyle she'd been falling into with Dex was normal for kids her age—that it was fun to have a few drinks and forget about the worries and concerns that everyone tried to heap on you.

But sometimes she had an unsettling feeling that she didn't quite fit in here, even though she tried, even though she might want to fit in around Dex and his friends. She was surprised that she was even having these thoughts tonight, of all nights, after the crazy day that she'd had. She definitely wanted to drink enough so that she could put that all aside until tomorrow. She got up to get herself another drink and go find Dex, who seemed to have disappeared on her for about the tenth time that evening.

She followed the hallway to the back room where people somehow seemed to congregate at the end of the night. She knocked lightly on the door and when no one answered she quietly pulled it open. Inside she could see Andrea, Dex, and Slade huddled up in the corner of the room around a low table. Dex looked up as she approached and reached for her hand, which she gave him as he pulled her over to sit on his lap. Andrea was just taking a needle out of her arm and Slade looked like he'd already had his fill of whatever the three of them had just done.

Jemma was drunk enough not to care but it was making her uneasy just the same. Dex leaned over to whisper in her ear.

"Do you wanna try it, babe? It will make you feel so much better."

He was rubbing her hand and trying to kiss her.

Jemma wasn't even sure why she was so confident in her response. If there was ever a night that she was tempted, it seemed like that moment would be now, but she wasn't. Not at all. Drunk, out of it, and slightly high on the joint she'd smoked with Dex earlier, yes, but suddenly she just knew that she wanted to be home in her bed.

She pulled Dex in for a hug before she stood up.

"I'm gonna go, babe. I'll call a cab."

"Stay the night," Dex asked, but he kind of looked

like he didn't care much one way or the other.

Jemma was sure that he was so out of it, he wouldn't even remember her leaving.

"No. I'll talk to you tomorrow, okay?" She leaned over to give him a quick kiss on the cheek. "Be good."

"You know it, babe." Dex laughed and Jemma went outside to get some fresh air and call the cab.

All of a sudden, she felt that she couldn't get out of the small apartment fast enough. It had all been too much—her whole day. She just needed a good night's sleep. And maybe something to eat, she thought as her stomach grumbled, reminding her that she'd forgotten to grab something to eat before she'd come to the party.

PAULA KAY

CHAPTER 6

Jemma had been up in her room avoiding Chase all morning. She didn't want to risk talking to him before she'd seen her mother and grandmother, who were finally due home any minute. She felt so many different emotions still, but mostly she felt sick to her stomach, which probably wasn't helped by all of the vodka she'd had to drink the night before. The anger and shock of what she'd learned still hadn't quite sunk in, and she knew deep down that the full scope of the truth yet to come wouldn't be felt until she could hear what her mother had to say to her.

She nearly jumped off the bed when she heard the garage door opening, announcing that the airport limo was probably up the driveway by now. Next she could hear the chatter of Kylie getting out of the car, which made her smile. Two minutes later she heard the young girl's footsteps bounding up the stairs to Jemma's room.

"Jemma, Jemma. Jemma, where are you?"

Jemma laughed, despite how nervous she felt.

"Where do you think I am, silly girl?"

One second later her bedroom door flung open and Kylie came running over to where Jemma was sitting on the bed, nearly knocking her over with a big hug.

"Good grief, Ky. You're like a giant puppy with no manners. The next thing I know, you're going to be licking my face."

Kylie stuck out her tongue and made a move towards Jemma's cheek to indicate that she was going to do just that.

Jemma laughed and grabbed her in a hug. "Very funny, twerp."

"You're a twerp." Kylie teased her back, laughing and giving her a big hug. "Jemma, I missed you so much."

"You did? What did you miss about me?"

Jemma was teasing her now—a game they often played.

Kylie was ready for it as she sat up on the bed to tick off on her fingers.

"Well, first I missed having coffee with you in the morning."

Jemma was nodding her head. "Okay, so of course you mean me having coffee and you having hot cocoa."

Kylie nodded. "Yes, of course, but shh. It's my turn still."

God, this child was funny. Jemma often wondered when they would hit the point where the little girl drove her crazy—like what had happened to so many of her friends with little sisters and brothers—but it just never had. She genuinely enjoyed Kylie's company and never seemed to tire of her. She was smiling at her now.

"Go on, then. Continue. Number two?"

"Number two is that I spent one afternoon doing an art project—oh, that's your surprise that I have to get from Grandma—oh, but that I missed you doing the art with me because you're so much better at it than Grandma." She whispered the last part, which made Jemma laugh even harder.

"Okay, and your third and final thing that you missed about me while you were gone?"

Kylie pretended she had to think about it, which Jemma knew was a joke, because she picked the same thing every time for the third thing. Jemma reached over to tickle her.

"The third thing, Ky. Out with it."

Kylie giggled. "The third thing I missed is you singing the song with me about the world being so small."

"It is, after all." Jemma winked.

"Grandma tried to sing it with me, but she doesn't know all the words."

"Who's talking about me in here?"

Jemma and Kylie both looked up to see their grandmother's head popping in the door and Jemma felt sick all over again.

"Never mind, Grandma," Kylie said, laughing. "Hey, can I get that thing please?"

"Hay is for horses, my dear. What thing are you

referring to?"

"You know. What I made for me and Jemma. Grandma, it's in your purse, remember?" Kylie seemed slightly exasperated as she waited for Linda to rummage around in her bag.

"Ky, be polite." Jemma couldn't help herself.

"Please, Grandma," Kylie added, smiling at Jemma.

Linda took a little plastic bag out of her purse and handed it to the little girl.

"Okay, you two. I'm going to go get myself organized."

Jemma cleared her throat, her heart beating faster. "Grandma."

Linda looked at her.

"I'd like to talk to you and Mom in a little while—if you could let her know, please."

Linda looked a little strange to Jemma, but she couldn't know, could she? Then again, maybe if one were hiding a secret this big for so many years, there had been numerous times when she thought the truth was coming—always waiting, wondering if something would be revealed.

"Okay, dear. You just let us know, then."

Linda leaned over to kiss both Kylie and Jemma on their foreheads before leaving them alone in Jemma's bedroom.

"Okay, so what is this surprise that you have for me, my dear sister?"

And like a punch to the gut, the words hit her. She hadn't thought of it before. How could she not have? She felt the tears come to her eyes and she tried to keep it together—but God. Kylie was not even the sister that she'd adored all these years. It was like the pieces of her family—the world that she'd known her whole life—were crashing down one by one, some fast, some slow—but soon she felt she'd be left with nothing. No truth or all of the truth about who she really was.

"Earth to Jemma."

Jemma looked at Kylie's little fingers snapping in front of her face. "Sorry, Ky. What were you saying?"

"Well, I was saying that it's funny that you should mention that I am your dear sister…" Kylie's hand disappeared into the plastic bag as Jemma sat there thinking about the complete irony of the conversation that they were having.

Kylie pulled out a beaded necklace with a flourish. "Hold out your hand."

Jemma obeyed, holding her hand out palm up.

Kylie placed the dainty beaded necklace in Jemma's hand and then pulled out an identical one to hold up and show her sister. "See, Jemma. It says 'my sister, my best friend.' And I have one too." Kylie was grinning from ear to ear, and Jemma was wiping her eyes quickly so that the little girl wouldn't see the tears that had appeared. "Jemma, I painted them. Grandma helped me. Do you like it?"

Jemma pulled her in for a big hug. "Ky, I love it. It's so beautiful. Thank you."

Kylie grinned and hugged her back.

"Now I think you better go say hello to your dad. I'm sure he's been missing you at least as much as I have."

Kylie got up off the bed. "Probably more," she said with a serious look on her face.

"Nah." Jemma tickled her one last time before giving her a little shove on her bottom toward the door. "Now scoot. We'll play later, okay?"

"Okay."

Jemma closed the door after Kylie left the room, immediately bursting into tears. She sat on her bed for a good ten minutes just holding the beaded necklace and thinking about her sister. So many emotions were coming up for her, but she was feeling more and more angry—like everything she'd ever known was just being pulled out from under her. And for the first time, she realized that it wasn't going to affect just her, but also Kylie. And what did her sister do to deserve anything but the truth in her life?

Jemma shook her head as if it could help shake some of these feelings from her before she walked into her bathroom to splash cold water on her face. She needed to get it together. From her bedroom window she could see that Kylie and Chase were outside playing catch. She took a deep breath, knowing that now was as good a time as any to confront her mother.

She reached into her nightstand drawer to take out the birth certificate from where she'd put it the day before. From the upstairs landing, she could hear both her mom and grandmother in the office downstairs. *How fitting.* Her mom was going to wish that she'd never asked her to go into her office for those stupid figures the other day.

Jemma descended the stairs, walked down the hallway toward the office, and took a deep breath before she stood in the doorway, holding the piece of paper up in front of her where her mother was sure to see it.

Blu looked up from where she was sitting behind her desk, her smile wide until she saw Jemma. And then Jemma had never seen her mom look so pale.

CHAPTER 7

At the same time as Blu stood up from her chair,
Jemma burst into tears. She really meant to hold it
together. She'd told herself over and over not to cry—at
least until she'd said what she'd needed to say, yet here
she was sobbing. And there was nothing she could do
now but fall into her mother's arms as she hurried across
the room to Jemma. Out of the corner of her eye, she saw
her grandmother, waiting in the corner chair—waiting for
what, she wasn't sure, but time would tell.

Jemma disengaged herself from her mother's arms in
a panic as if she'd not allow one more second of closeness
between them. She pulled away and stared at her. Finally
she cleared her throat.

"How could you? Both of you?"

Her mother looked like she was in complete shock,
and her grandmother was a deer caught in headlights,
reminding Jemma of another time long ago when she'd
first laid eyes on her. It was a flash of memory that
surprised her, but of course now everything made sense.
She was young then, so she couldn't really piece it all

together; but knowing what she knew now, she understand her mother's urgency in keeping the two of them apart back then. And she'd almost succeeded.

"Jemma."

Her mom was sobbing now too, looking toward her grandmother—for what, Jemma wasn't sure. She already understood why it had all happened the way it had. Her grandmother had shared parts of her past with Jemma— told her that she'd not been fit to raise Jemma's mother, so it made perfect sense that she wouldn't have been able to raise another baby. Jemma understood all of that— intellectually. She only didn't understand why they had kept if from her for so long.

She glared at her mother. "Do you have any idea how betrayed I feel? The fact that you've both been lying to me all this time—all my life."

"Jemma, I didn't—" Blu looked over at her mother— at *their* mother, who looked just as shocked—"we didn't know how or when—or we didn't know what would be best for you." Her mother looked stunned. "That's not exactly true. I decided and Grandma only agreed to what I'd asked of her."

Jemma couldn't believe that she could possibly feel any more shocked than she'd already felt, but standing here hearing her mother say the words—it only made things worse, not better. She didn't feel better at all. She walked over to sit on the sofa, sighing deeply as she put her face in her hands.

Finally she looked up at both of them as they stood watching her, not speaking—probably just as much at a loss for words as Jemma was. What was there to say? What could they possibly say?

"What am I supposed to do now?"

She felt the tears still coming and she didn't care as she waited for her mother to speak.

"I don't know what to tell you, Jemma. Does anything have to change? I mean, I know it's shocking and it will take some getting used to, but it doesn't change anything." She looked down and then over to Jemma with a look that spoke of all the pleading that Jemma guessed must be in her heart at that moment. "Jemma, I've always loved you like a daughter. That's all you've ever been to me. You do understand that, don't you?"

Jemma nodded her head slowly, but looked toward her grandmother. "What about how you feel? How you've felt all these years? I can't believe—I just can't believe that you're my mother." And then she turned toward her mother. "And my sister. It's crazy, you know?"

They were both nodding their heads. Yes, they did know. It was all coming out, just as Jemma was sure that her mom suspected it might during all these years. It was a small miracle that she hadn't found out before now, and somewhat fitting that it was just before her eighteenth birthday.

Her grandmother cleared her throat.

"Jemma, I agreed to keep your mom's secret because I understood. It was a consequence of a past that I needed to move on from—not that I wanted to move on from the two of you, but we—your mother and I—needed a way to move forward together, for all of us. It doesn't change anything. You were born my daughter, yes, but Blu hasn't loved you any less than I have. Certainly she's given you a better life than I ever could have—back then, anyway. When it really counted. I'm grateful to her for that and no matter what happens—no matter how you feel towards us—I'll always know that she made the right decision in taking you from me all those years ago."

Jemma was nodding her head. She understood. She wanted to scream at them. She wasn't stupid. She did understand everything, but still, she had been lied to for so incredibly long. Way too long. That was the part that she was having a hard time dealing with. That was the part that she was so angry about.

Just then, Kylie came running into the room squealing, with Chase not far behind.

"Finally. I can't believe I've not seen you all weekend, young lady." Chase winked at Jemma, but just as quickly looked toward Blu once he saw Jemma's face.

The room was shockingly quiet, all except for the singing of Kylie off in the corner.

"Kylie, will you please go take your backpack up to your room," said Blu.

Kylie looked up as if to argue, but then seemed to think better of it as she bounded out of the room, stopping to give her dad a quick kiss on the cheek on the way out.

Chase looked from one to the other of them before his eyes settled on Blu, who nodded at him.

"Jemma knows. She found her birth certificate."

Jemma didn't know why but she didn't want Chase to talk to her. She didn't want to know his thoughts about it. He was another one who had kept the secret from her. But Chase didn't read her body language correctly; he got up to cross the room, putting his arm around her shoulders as he sat next to her on the couch. She shrugged it off.

"Don't. Please." Jemma wiped her eyes with the back of her hand. She looked around the room at each of them, these people that she had trusted for most of her life. Her mother whom she'd never had a reason not to trust—to believe in. They'd been through so much together. She looked around the room and she didn't know any of them. There was a wall between them now. It surrounded them and left her on the outs and in that moment, it was just the way she wanted it. She didn't want anything to do with this family of hers.

PAULA KAY

CHAPTER 8

Jemma willed Dex to pick up his phone.

Please pick up, please pick up.

"Hi, babe, what's up?"

"Dex. I need to get out of here."

"You want me to come pick you up?"

"Yeah, but like I mean I'm leaving here. For good."
She was crying now, but she knew she couldn't stay. She'd
never really thought of running away before but she was
practically eighteen anyway.

"Are you talking about my text?"

"No, what text? What are you talking about?"

She pulled up her text messages while listening to Dex
on the speakerphone.

Babe, let's go to LA. Andrea says we can stay with her.

"No, I hadn't seen your text until now."

"That's kind of crazy, Jem."

"Yeah, well, my life has suddenly become a little
crazy, hasn't it? Yes, let's do it. Let's go to LA. Will you
pick me up later? When I text you? I'm going to wait until
everyone is asleep. No need for more drama than what

has already taken place today."

Dex agreed that he'd be waiting for her text, and Jemma hung up the phone feeling more calm than she'd felt in the last two days—maybe even in the last few months. It was time for her to be on her own, to do things on her terms. It might be hard for the first few weeks, but she'd be with Dex and then—she'd get her money—the trust.

And she already knew that there wasn't anything anyone could do to keep that from her. Douglas had explained to her how it all worked, and she understood that Arianna had set it up so that she would have full control of the money once she turned eighteen. For some reason Arianna had trusted that Jemma would be a smart girl at eighteen—that she'd have the wherewithal to know how to handle all that money. Arianna hadn't known that Jemma would be as messed up as she was.

Jemma thought there was a certain amount of irony to the whole thing because from everything she knew about Arianna, when she was eighteen, she wasn't all that different than Jemma—the poor little rich girl, trying to figure out what in life was more important than the next party or getting drunk.

But Arianna had changed. Everyone had seen it. Everyone would talk about it for years to come, and even though Jemma couldn't remember everything about Ari, she remembered the important parts—how much Arianna had loved her and that Jemma had been important to her.

Jemma thought about going into Kylie's room to see if she wanted to play a game or something, but then at the last minute she knew she couldn't bear to do that to her. Instead, she crawled under her covers and waited for the house to go dark.

She debated about leaving a note, but in the end, she just grabbed the backpack and her purse—tucking a few last things into the pockets—the necklace from Kylie, her phone and a small stack of photos she kept in the drawer of her desk. She removed the house key from her key ring, placing it on her dresser—making a statement, she supposed.

When Dex texted her that he was down the street, she quietly slipped down the hallway, at the last minute putting her things down outside of Kylie's door to go in and give her a gentle kiss on her forehead.

She slipped out the front door, put her backpack on, and walked down the driveway without looking back.

PAULA KAY

CHAPTER 9

Jemma sat up quickly, nearly knocking her head on the coffee table she seemed to practically be sleeping under. It took her a full minute to remember where she was and why she was sleeping on the floor alongside about a dozen other people. Her stomach lurched as she stood up to make her way to find a bathroom. *God, how much did I have to drink last night?* She rubbed her head, trying to recall what had happened after she and Dex had arrived in LA.

She remembered being freezing cold by the time they'd made the two-hour trip on Dex's motorcycle. And then, once they'd gotten close, they had a horrible time finding the apartment, as Andrea's directions scribbled on a napkin for Dex hadn't gotten them anywhere remotely close to where she was living. Jemma remembered feeling extremely frustrated by the time they finally arrived at the apartment and the party that was in full swing at three o'clock in the morning.

There was no sleeping at that point. Besides, after the day that she'd had, she needed a drink or two and welcomed the shots of vodka being thrust into her hand by Andrea. She vaguely remembered Andrea giving her a tour of the place, but now that she was up in the light of day she couldn't remember it at all.

After finding the bathroom—and stepping over someone who'd apparently passed out while being sick in the toilet—she had a look around as she made her way to the kitchen with hopes of finding some coffee to make. The place was filthy. She couldn't help thinking it. She tried to talk herself out of being so judgmental—after all, not everyone had grown up with housekeepers and a mother who was a slightly neurotic neat freak—but the place looked like it hadn't been cleaned in weeks.

The kitchen wasn't any better than the bathroom and living room she'd just walked through, and she was sure that the party last night had added to the massive stack of dishes and open containers of food that she saw everywhere. She opened a few cupboards in the hopes of finding some coffee to go with the semi-used-looking coffee pot she found in the corner on the kitchen counter. Nothing. Finally she thought to open the freezer and found one little bit of a bag of generic coffee. Perfect.

She stared out at the living room while she waited for the coffee to brew. She couldn't even make out Dex's body in the sea of bodies lying around the living room sofas and floor. Good grief. It looked like a scene out of some comedy movie involving frat boys and girls gone wild. People were in various states of dress and she noticed at least a couple of girls without their tops on. God help her if she ever woke up half naked in a room full of people.

She filled a cup that she'd washed from the sink, and after taking a tentative whiff of the milk from the refrigerator decided that this might be the day that she started drinking her coffee black.

Just as she was debating where she should try to find someplace to sit, she saw Andrea enter the hallway from the bathroom.

"Oh, hey. You're up early," Andrea said, looking a bit crazy and disheveled. "That was some rager last night. I'm so glad you and Dex made it."

"I guess so. I can't even remember half of it, to be honest. And my head is hurting me." Jemma laughed lightly, feeling slightly awkward now in this strange place with someone she barely knew. "I hope you don't mind. I really needed some caffeine and I found some in the freezer. There's plenty there if you want a cup."

Andrea was shaking her head as she opened the refrigerator to pull out a can of beer. "Not until after I have at least two of these. For some reason that always seems to help my hangover." She laughed and then started coughing uncontrollably. When she could finally speak, she started walking across the room, motioning for Jemma to follow. "We can sit out on the balcony."

"Great." Jemma followed her out onto a very small balcony with two worn lawn chairs and a plastic table.

Andrea flipped open a pack of cigarettes that she'd grabbed off the table on her way out, offering one to Jemma.

"No thanks. I need to just sip some of this coffee first." Jemma looked out, accessing her surroundings for the first time in the light of day. She was definitely far from her home on the beach. She felt a quick pang of something inside her. Regret? She brushed it aside.

Andrea lit up and took a long drag as she seemed to be studying Jemma. "So, Dex says you've left home for good then?"

"Yeah, well, that's the plan." Jemma didn't know why exactly, but she felt like crying. And she really didn't feel like discussing her problems with Andrea at the moment.

"Well, you guys can stay here for awhile. There's four of us here right now, but you're welcome to the sofas. And then it would be great if you could pitch in some rent money in a few days too."

Jemma thought Andrea seemed to be eyeing her with some skepticism.

"Yeah, for sure." But just as fast as the words were out of her mouth, she realized that she didn't have more than forty dollars on her. Chase had always given her cash each week as part of her allowance, and she really hadn't even stopped to think about what she was going to do about money until her birthday next month—until the trust went into effect. She wouldn't worry about that now. Dex usually had plenty of cash on him and she didn't ask questions about where it came from.

"So, I know your family is rich and everything, but Dex says that you're about to inherit a bunch of money. Next month, is it?"

Wow. Jemma really couldn't believe that Dex had told this girl who was a stranger to her about her trust. How annoying. She wondered for a moment why he'd done so, but just as quickly put it down to his just telling the info as if it was something to know about his girlfriend. She had never really gotten the impression that he cared so much about her money, but time would tell, she guessed. Money did strange things to relationships. She'd seen that a bit with her mother over the years as old friendships faded away for new ones to take their place.

She turned her attention back to Andrea. "Yeah, I'm going to get a bit of money when I turn eighteen." She saw the question on Andrea's face. "It's from an old friend of the family's—I knew her when I was very young."

"That's pretty fantastic." Andrea took a big puff on her cigarette. "It must be nice."

Jemma looked up at her as she continued.

"To not have to worry about anything, I mean."

"Well, I wouldn't say that. I definitely have my share of problems right now. Problems that won't be solved by money," she added.

Andrea seemed to be eyeing her with that look again. If Jemma were being skeptical, she'd swear the girl was judging her—which seemed a bit ludicrous to her, considering Andrea's own apparent circumstances.

"Well, you don't seem like someone who has many problems to me." Andrea seemed to be forcing a laugh.

"Well, looks can be deceiving." Jemma sighed. She really wanted to change the subject and talk about something other than herself. "So what do you usually do for fun around here?"

"Oh, you know. See what the guys are up to—once everyone wakes up, which by the looks of things could be many hours from now. At some point I have to go out and make some money." Andrea laughed. "Rent is coming due soon and right now I've got maybe fifty bucks."

Jemma swore that the look Andrea was giving her was daring her to ask questions.

"Oh, so what do you do? For work, I mean?"

Andrea took a swig of her beer. "You mean Dex didn't tell you?"

Jemma shook her head. "No, honestly, Dex and I haven't had much of a chance to talk about much these past few days at all."

"Well, let's just say that I do what I have to do."

There was that look again. Jemma tried to imagine what she was insinuating and wondered if she should press further. Andrea seemed to be enjoying her discomfort—as if she wanted to talk about it—perhaps wanting to make their apparent differences that much more known. Jemma would take the bait.

She took a sip of her coffee and tried to make her voice sound nonchalant. "So, what exactly does that mean? Are you some big drug dealer or something?" She laughed, trying to make the point that she was joking.

Andrea laughed. "I wish. That would be easy money."

Jemma waited for her to continue.

"Okay, not really, but it's not something I'd turn down if I got into the right circles. So far, that's not really happened—what with these lowlifes I've been hanging around."

Jemma thought the description of Andrea's so-called friends seemed ironic, but then again maybe that was how Andrea meant it. It was funny because even though her impression of the girl hadn't been great, she had the distinct feeling that she was very smart. Not unlike what her mom and Chase were constantly telling Jemma—that she needed to push more to live up to her potential, to her talents. Jemma shook her head as if that could remove the thoughts she was suddenly having about her family.

She turned her attention back to Andrea. "Okay, so what are you saying? You have a pimp or something?"

"No. God, no. Well, no pimp anyway. I've tried hard to avoid that because I've got a few friends that have gotten themselves into some shady situations." She eyed Jemma before she continued. "But you know. I do things on my own terms. Only when it works for me. And it's not like I'm standing out on the street corners or anything. At least that's a rare occasion." She laughed lightly.

God, so she was prostituting herself. Jemma really didn't know what to think, but it made her feel sick all of the sudden. She was trying to keep a straight face because at this point, after only just arriving at Andrea's, she didn't need the girl to think that she was there to be a judgmental prude or anything.

"Okay. And you think that is safe?" Jemma finally managed.

"Yeah. Well, as safe as anything these days, I guess." Andrea laughed again, taking a final gulp of her beer. "Mostly the guys I'm with are people I kinda know." She looked over, and Jemma guessed she could see the question on her face without her having to ask it. "You know—a word-of-mouth kinda thing."

Andrea stood up then and opened the screen door to the inside of the apartment. "Look, Jemma. I don't mind you being here, but I really don't wanna feel like you're living off of us for free and I certainly don't wanna feel like you're better than me—better than all of us."

Jemma was taken aback as to where Andrea's words—her feelings—were coming from. She really hadn't thought that she'd said anything that could be construed as judgmental—well, not out loud anyway. She turned slightly in her chair to face Andrea. "No, Andrea. You got it wrong. I don't feel that way. Not at all." *But do I?* "And of course I expect to contribute rent money. Dex and I both will. You don't need to worry about that, okay?"

Andrea nodded her head. "Okay." She seemed thoughtful for a few seconds. "Look, I'm sorry. I can get a little defensive sometimes. And sometimes, a lot of stuff goes on in my head. I do like you. So I'm not sure where all that came from. My own issues, I suppose." She laughed lightly. "Let's just forget I said any of that okay."

Jemma nodded her head. "No worries."

And then she was alone on the balcony.

PAULA KAY

CHAPTER 10

Jemma only had a few minutes to herself after Andrea left the balcony before Dex was out there thrusting her ringing phone at her.

"Dude, your phone's been ringing off the hook." Dex coughed and Jemma thought he looked the roughest she'd ever seen him.

"Dude?" Jemma laughed.

"Yeah, dude." Dex laughed and leaned over as if to try to kiss Jemma.

Jemma leaned far back from him before his lips could make contact with her.

"Dude, I think you better go brush your teeth first." She laughed but she was thinking that they both could use a shower sooner rather than later.

"Well, aren't you Little Miss High and Mighty this morning? You weren't complaining about my kisses last night." Dex sat down in the chair next to her, pulling a cigarette out from the pack in his jeans pocket.

Jemma leaned over to brush her lips across Dex's cheek. "Is that so? I hardly remember, to be honest." She eyed him as he took a long puff from his cigarette. "I'm not sure that we should be partying like that every night. Just to be clear."

Dex gave her a long look, and the stern line of his mouth didn't flinch. "Babe, I don't need a mother, okay? I'm totally cool with what Andrea and these guys have going on here. If you're not…"

Jemma felt like she'd been punched in the gut. "If I'm not, then what?"

"Well. I'm just saying—no one is going to force you to stay here. You can always go running back home to Mommy."

Jemma took a deep breath. She really wanted to lighten the mood. She punched Dex lightly on the arm. "Hey, I'm cool. You don't need to worry about me going home—or going anywhere right now for that matter. Look, I'm sorry. Forget I said anything, okay, babe?"

She hated how she sounded. When had she started sounding so apologetic? So needy?

Dex leaned over to kiss her full on the lips. "Good."

Jemma kissed him back while at the same time stopping his hand from traveling further than where it was already placed on the inside of her thigh. "Easy there, tiger. We've got a bit of an audience stirring inside."

Dex gave her one more hard kiss and relented as he sat back to finish his cigarette.

Jemma sipped the last of her coffee as she looked through her missed calls and texts. She had ten missed calls from her mother, three from Chase, and three from her grandmother. Her heart beat fast as she noticed the name Gram on her phone. What did she even call her grandmother now—Linda? It was all still so surreal. She could see that she also had messages but she wasn't quite ready to hear her mother's voice. Instead, she started flipping through her texts, which had begun to come in around six o'clock that morning.

Her mom had texted first.

Jemma, this isn't funny. Where are you?

Followed by a text from Chase twenty minutes later.

J, call your mother. Not cool.

There were a few more after that, and then Jemma detected a distinct change in the tone of her mother's notes.

Jemma, please. I'm so sorry but we can work this out. Please call me as soon as you get this. Honey, we're worried about you. I need to know that you're okay. Please, Jemma.

Jemma sighed. She would phone her back. She just needed to be alone with her thoughts for a few more minutes. Suddenly she didn't know what she felt about anything. She just knew she felt bad and confused over everything that had happened.

She noticed Dex staring at her as she put her phone down on the table between them.

"So? Are you gonna call her?'

"Yeah. I will. I just need a minute to figure out what I'm gonna say." She eyed him, trying to decide if it was worth having a conversation about anything serious with him at that time. "I mean, what are we gonna do?"

"About?"

"About staying here, Dex. They don't exactly have tons of room and Andrea does want rent money, you know."

"Okay, so we'll get some money together. I'm sure that you can get your mom and Chase to put some into your account, can't you? And don't you have any of your allowance left?"

Jemma was shaking her head. "No, I don't." She looked carefully at Dex before she continued. "I'm not sure why you think they're going to give me any money right now. That seems doubtful."

Dex looked exasperated. "Oh, please. They're not gonna let their baby girl starve."

Jemma didn't like the tone of his voice when he talked about her parents—which seemed kinda crazy to her, given her own feelings toward them, but she knew he was wrong about them giving her money. It wouldn't be that easy. If it were just her mother maybe, but Chase would draw a harder line. She was sure of that.

"I dunno, Dex. How much money do you have?"

"Not much, really. Maybe I can get a hundred dollars out." Dex laughed. "Okay, so we'll have to figure out how we're gonna earn our keep around here." He brought his hand up Jemma's leg again. "I'm sure there are ways."

Jemma pushed his hand away harder than she'd

intended. "What are you saying? And by the way, do you know what exactly Andrea does to make money? Because I just found out this morning." Her heart was beating faster in her chest as she waited for his reply.

"I know exactly what Andrea does and yes, that's what I'm saying. I'm sure you could make double or triple the money she makes." He was running his fingers through Jemma's hair. "You're so much prettier, babe."

Jemma turned quickly in her chair, knocking Dex's hand away from her hair. "Are you serious right now? Tell me you're joking." She was fighting the tears that threatened to fall any second.

Dex gave her a funny look. "Why not? Don't be such a prude. I know you won't give it up for me, but it would be an easy way to make the money that we need to stay here. In LA, I mean—just until you get your trust money."

Jemma was on her feet. "Dex, I'm not going to start having sex with strange guys—or any guys for that matter—for money. I can't believe you're even considering asking me to do that." She was crying now.

Dex pulled her down into his lap, holding her tight as she fought to get back up.

"Hey, chill out babe. It was just an idea." He kissed her on the cheek.

She wiped the tears from her face with her hand as she turned to look at him. "I wouldn't do that, you know. Ever."

"I know. You don't have to. We'll figure something out."

Jemma thought he was acting like he never meant it in the first place, but she knew that he was trying to feel her out about the idea—that he'd definitely let her go with other men if she were willing. She felt sick to her stomach and suddenly like she was in a bit over her head—with running away, with Dex, with Andrea here in this strange apartment. She sighed as she finally stopped resisting sitting on Dex's lap and laid back against him. She'd figure it all out later—maybe when she phoned her mom back.

Dex pushed her off his lap as he attempted to stand up. "Babe, I need a drink. Do you want one?" He headed in toward the apartment.

"Yes please." She wanted to be drunk—to forget everything for a while. Or at least to get a few drinks in her in order to relax a bit before she called her mom.

Dex called to her from inside the screen door. "I'll bring it out to you. Vodka and orange juice?"

"Yeah, if they have it. I'm not so sure though, so if not, I'll have it straight."

Dex was giving her a look. "Starting pretty early today, aren't we?" He laughed.

"So now you're judging me on my drink selection." Jemma laughed too, happy that things seemed to be a little lighter between her and Dex. She needed him now. She needed someone who was on her side. Dex did seem to be—when it suited him. She couldn't help the thought that came quickly.

She leaned back against the chair and picked up her phone again while she waited for Dex to return with her drink. Was she in over her head? She really hadn't thought any of this through. Even though it had been rough going between her and her mom lately, she'd never actually thought about running away. She wasn't stupid. She knew she had a good thing going there—that her mom and Chase wanted her to have everything. Not just material things, but things that would give her a good life. She sighed as Dex handed her the small half glass of what looked like straight vodka.

"Thanks. No OJ, I take it?"

"Nope." He was turning to go back inside. "I'm gonna go lie down on that space that just opened up on the couch. Coming?"

"No, I think I'll sit here awhile longer." Dex was eyeing the phone in her hand. "I'm gonna call my mom in a few minutes. I need to just get it over with."

"Okay. Well, try to get some money out of them." Dex winked as he turned to go inside.

Alone again, Jemma finally punched in the code on her phone that would let her listen to all of the messages that had been left for her.

PAULA KAY

CHAPTER 11

Blu's messages to Jemma seemed to grow in intensity—and fear, Jemma thought as she listened to them. By the tenth message, her mom sounded frightened and Jemma knew that she needed to at least text her. She pulled up the last text from her mother and bit her lip as she tried to decide how much to tell her.

I'm okay. With Dex.

Just keep it simple—reach out to let her know that she wasn't dead in a ditch somewhere. She clicked the button to send it off and within seconds received a text back.

Where are you? Call me please.

Jemma sighed as she texted back.

We're in LA. Stayin at a friend's.

LA? I'm calling. Answer the phone please.

Jemma debated about not answering her phone when it rang a second later. She'd have to talk to her mom sooner or later. She just wanted to have an idea of what she was gonna say—what she was feeling about everything.

"Hi, Mom—or should I be calling you Blu now?" She couldn't help the anger that was right there again just like that.

"Jemma. Listen to me. You need to come home so that we can talk about this—work everything out."

"Yeah, well, I just don't see what we're going to be able to work out at all. Do you? Honestly?"

Jemma was trying to hold back her tears, angry at herself for feeling so upset yet again. She didn't want her mom to think that she was anything other than okay.

Her mother was quiet for a few seconds on the other end of the phone. "Jemma." Jemma heard her take a deep breath and could picture Blu standing near the kitchen in the breakfast room, looking out toward the view of the ocean. "Jemma, I—we never meant to hurt you. You gotta believe that. I only ever wanted what was best for you—because I-I love you, Jemma. I always have. You know that, right?"

Jemma was crying now because she did know that. Deep down, she could never doubt how much she'd been loved, but it didn't excuse the lies. Did it? Not when she was old enough to understand anyway. It was just all so twisted—so wrong.

"Jemma? Are you there?"

"Yes. I'm here," Jemma managed, willing her tears to stop. "I just don't know."

"Jemma, come home. Just come home. We can't fix any of this if you're not here. And God, Jemma—I—

we're all worried about you. LA isn't the glamorous place that you guys have probably made it out to be. It can be dangerous."

"God, Mom. I know that." Just like that, Jemma was back to feeling angry. Her mother treated her like such a child, and that drove her crazy.

"I know. I didn't mean anything by it. I just want you to come home, okay?"

Jemma wasn't ready to go home yet. But she wasn't quite ready to let her mom know that.

"Mom? I-I could use some money. There wasn't any in my account when I left and now we—I don't even have enough for food and stuff."

There was silence on the other end of the line as she waited for her mom to answer. Blu wasn't stupid, but Jemma knew that the idea of her with no money would get to her mom. She was counting on it.

"Mom, please. Just like a couple hundred dollars or something?"

"Well, are you coming home then? If I put two hundred in your account, you'll use it to get home? As in today, Jemma—hold on. Chase wants to talk to you."

God. Chase wasn't going to let it happen. Jemma knew that he was much harder to convince of anything.

"Jemma, what are you doing? You've gotten your mom and grandma frantic here. You do know that, don't you?"

Chase sounded irritated, and Jemma pictured her

mother there tugging at his arm, giving him a stern look that told him to cool it.

"How do you think I feel right now?" Jemma could hold her own during her arguments with Chase. Well, she liked to think so anyway, even though it seemed like she rarely got her way with him, but she could be just as stubborn. That was for sure.

"I know. I'm sorry."

Chase's voice got softer—less stern.

"I know you've been through a lot. No one is denying that. But Jemma, you can't just run away from your problems—from us."

There was silence for a few seconds and Jemma imagined that her mom was talking to Chase.

"Look, we'll transfer one hundred fifty to your account when we hang up. And will you be home today?"

Jemma wasn't going home. Not yet.

"Yes. Thank you."

"Okay, I'm counting on you to hold up your end of the deal. We're counting on you being at home in your bed tonight so that we can all get up tomorrow and work this out. Jemma?"

"Yeah, I heard you."

She hated begging. Only until next month, she thought. Then she'd be eighteen. She'd have the trust money. She wouldn't need to answer to any of them. Surely they realized that. It was almost laughable. Their window of time to control her—through money or anything, really—was closing and Jemma just needed to wait it out a little longer.

She turned her attention back to Chase on the other end of the line.

"Okay, I gotta go. Thanks for the money."

"Jemma, wait—Kylie wants to talk to you."

"No—I—"

But it was too late. Jemma could hear her little sister crying already.

"Jemma?"

Jemma took a deep breath. She wouldn't lie to her sister. She couldn't just lie and make everything better—make everything go away.

"Hi, Ky. Don't cry."

"When are you coming back?" The little girl seemed to manage her words through her sobs so that Jemma could still make them out.

"I don't know. But don't tell that to Mom and Chase, okay?" Jemma needed to be careful. It wasn't fair to put her sister in the middle.

"Jemma. I don't want you to be gone. I miss you."

Kylie was crying again and Jemma thought her heart would break.

"I know. I miss you too. Ky, everything's gonna be okay. I'm sure that I'll see you soon."

"Promise?"

When would she see the little girl? For the first time since Jemma had started the phone call with her mother, she was feeling a twinge of regret. She couldn't live without Kylie in her life. Could she? It seemed unbearable. But what was the alternative? She couldn't see one—at least not until she was living on her own— legitimately, in a way that her mom and Chase couldn't argue with. Maybe she'd buy a place in San Diego on the beach and they'd let Kylie come stay with her on the weekends. She turned her attention back to her sister on the other end of the line.

"I promise. Soon, Ky, okay? I love you. Will you put Mom back on the phone, please?"

"Okay, I love you too, Jemma."

Jemma wiped at her eyes as Blu came back on to say hello.

"I just wanted to say thanks for the money."

"It's okay. Just come home so we can fix this. I love—"

Jemma clicked off the phone, purposely cutting her mom off.

She needed a few more minutes alone to try to gather her thoughts. She wondered if she should tell Dex about the money her mom was going to transfer. For the first time since she'd known him, she had second thoughts when it came to them sharing information about their finances. Her instinct told her that she'd be wise to start keeping some of her business to herself—especially as her birthday drew nearer. Maybe she'd just tell him that she had enough in her account to get them some food, which was essentially true as the one fifty was not going to last them long in LA. This was even more true if she or Dex decided that they needed to use the money for partying, which was a definite possibility if last night was any indication of how the rest of the week would be playing out.

Jemma sighed. She was thinking too much. She was young and allowed to party a bit. She was acting like her mother, being all practical, something which she would try to avoid at all costs—especially right now when she pretty much couldn't stand her mother. She was actually a bit shocked at how easily the anger came to the surface when she'd talked to her.

Chase's words rang in her head. She *had* been through a lot. But somehow—with or without her mom—she was going to have to sort some things out for herself. She did realize this and hadn't completely lost her mind in all of her rage. At least this was true when she was sober anyway.

CHAPTER 12

Jemma held onto Dex as they rode his motorcycle to find an ATM machine. She'd checked her account online from her phone, and Blu had transferred the money within minutes of their conversation. She felt a twinge of something because she knew that she could always count on her mom when it came to keeping her word and coming through for her. It was ironic to think that for all of her life, she'd never trusted anyone as much as she'd trusted her mother. Yet, Blu had been keeping the biggest secret of all from her.

She held tighter to Dex as they rounded a corner going much faster than what Jemma was typically comfortable with.

"Hey, slow down there, mister. The last thing we need right now is for you to be getting a speeding ticket."

Also, her mom hadn't said anything about calling the police, but Jemma knew that it was something that they very well could do and might be tempted to do once they knew that she really wasn't coming home that day. Well, she didn't know if her mom would have it in her, but

Chase would definitely report her missing, if it meant Jemma would be forced to come home.

She'd have to cross that bridge when she came to it, but for now she and Dex needed to not have any run-ins with the police. She'd been lucky in that regard since hanging out with him and his friends. Every time that they'd gotten into some kind of trouble, she'd not been around him, so to date her record was clean, which was more than one could say about Dex's. But he hadn't gotten into any real trouble. Yet. She didn't know why, but having the thought seemed foreboding to her and she shook her head as if the motion was enough to will it from happening. She couldn't control Dex and she'd never try.

He laughed now as he squeezed her hand that had come around to his chest. "Hang on, baby."

"Dex!"

She wasn't in the mood to argue with him about his driving. She wasn't in the mood to argue with him about anything. She knew after her phone call with her mom and Chase that she needed Dex right now. She needed someone on her side and Dex was her someone.

He pulled up to the curb in front of an ATM machine and Jemma hopped off the back of the bike.

"How much are you getting, babe?"

Jemma bit her lip. "I was thinking just like fifty dollars—enough for dinner and maybe to buy a couple things for the apartment?"

"Well, how much do you have?"

Jemma looked at him, trying to decide how she felt about his asking.

"Not much. What else do we need and what about your account?"

"I'm broke right now. Gonna have to figure something out soon."

Jemma nodded her head, not saying out loud what she was thinking about Dex needing to get a real job at some point.

"I was just thinking that we should really contribute to the party Andrea and them are having tonight. I'm sure someone can go by the liquor store later if we give them some cash."

Jemma was in a weird space—not yet fully recovered from last night's hangover and still reeling with the emotions of everything that had happened. She knew that later that night her phone would be blowing up with texts and calls from her mom and Chase when she didn't turn up at home. She was suddenly sure that the only thing that would keep her sane was a good night of drinking. She sighed and turned back towards Dex. "Okay. You're right. I'll take out the whole one fifty. But can we go get some fast food or something after? I'm starving."

"Great, babe, and yes, I'm starving too."

Jemma took her helmet from Dex and climbed back on the motorcycle behind him.

"Dex?"

"Yeah?"

"I don't really wanna go back to Andrea's yet. Can we get some food and go to the beach?"

"Yep. That works for me. Do you wanna go get your bathing suit?"

"Nope. I just wanna walk around—or sit and look at the water. Andrea is great to let us stay there and everything—I'm not complaining—but don't you find it a little depressing?"

Dex turned his body a bit to look at her. "Sometimes you can be such a princess, Jem."

She hated it when he called her that.

"I'm not. Don't call me that."

"Well, not everyone has grown up like you have—fancy cars, houses, and schools."

"I know. Look, forget I said anything."

"I just—I don't like it when you're acting all better than everyone else—including me."

Jemma felt herself getting angry—like a switch had been turned on.

"Don't say that. It's not true. I'm not acting like that at all. I just don't wanna lie around a sad apartment all day with a bunch of drunk people." She stared at him intently. "And yes, that does include you—if that happens to be your plan for the day."

She felt unbelievably tired all of a sudden and her comfy bed at home flashed in her mind. She couldn't go home. Not yet. She needed to make things okay with Dex. Fighting with him was the last thing she needed right now.

"Look, forget it. You're right. I'm sorry. I'm just tired and I need some food in me." She gave Dex a tight squeeze and leaned in to kiss the back of his neck, hoping he'd just drop the conversation she no longer wanted to be having.

Dex turned slightly to kiss her on the lips. "Forgotten. Now let's go get some burgers."

They spent the next few hours at the beach. It was great for Jemma to be able to take her mind off of things for a while. She loved the ocean, and since they were both so tired, most of their time was spend taking a nap in a nice shaded area that they'd found in one of the parks near enough to see the water.

Jemma had gotten a few texts from her mother, asking her when to expect her at home. She'd not replied yet and she knew that if she didn't soon, her mom and Chase were going to become really furious with her. She was still trying to decide how to handle everything with them. One thing was certain. After today, she'd not be able to ask either of them for any money.

In the back of her mind, she had a thought that she could probably ask her grandmother. She could guilt-trip her into transferring some money to Jemma's account, but she knew it was risky. Her grandma would hate doing it behind Blu's back and she'd obviously have to do it without Blu knowing.

Jemma laughed lightly despite the seriousness of her thoughts. Heck, maybe she'd have to take Andrea up on her offer of prostitution after all. She cringed. God help her if she ever got that desperate. She hoped that she'd return home—or get a job in a restaurant—before she'd do something like that.

"What's so funny?"

Dex was stirring beside her in the grass, reaching out to pull her closer to him.

"Oh, nothing. Just thinking—and trying not to be stressed out."

Dex pulled her on top of him, giving her a deep kiss on the mouth. "I know how to help you be much less stressed, babe."

Jemma laughed but her heart was pounding. She was probably the only virgin among any of her friends—or anyone she was hanging out with—but for some reason she just had a check in her gut about giving it up for Dex. It didn't feel right to her. She couldn't help but think that her mother and Chase would be proud of her. Somehow whenever she'd talked about it with Blu, she had the feeling that her mom didn't really believe that it was true.

Jemma didn't know what or who she was saving herself for exactly but she did know that it wasn't going to happen in a public park, so that was an easy save. She laughed now as she kissed Dex back and tried to change the subject just as quickly. She rolled off him, taking his hand in her own.

"Do you wanna head back?"

He stared at her intently. Honestly, she was always a bit shocked at his patience when it came to sex. It had to be something he'd been taking—one of the drugs that Jemma didn't exactly know about—that had seemed to lessen his sex drive lately.

He nodded, standing and pulling her up along with him. "Yeah, let's go see what everyone is up to."

CHAPTER 13

Andrea had said that Jemma could chill in her room for a bit—a good thing, as Jemma could hear the party starting outside the door. She wasn't quite in the party mood just yet and relished the quiet time to herself.

She reached over to the bedside table to grab her phone, clicking the button to check for any new texts. She scrolled through about a dozen from her mom and several from Chase. They were angry, just as she knew that they would be. She would make up some excuse but she knew that they wouldn't be buying it.

She eyed the shot glass of liquor that Andrea had popped in with a few minutes ago with. She'd said it was for whenever Jemma was ready to come join the fun. Jemma was glad that Andrea didn't seem upset with her, and she'd figured that she'd be able to get back into her good graces at tonight's party if there was anything still lingering. She'd show Andrea and the others that she did know how to party and have a good time. Her thoughts turned toward her earlier conversation with Dex. And she'd show him that she didn't, in fact, think she was a princess at all.

She got up to change into her party clothes—old jeans and a t-shirt supporting one of the up-and-coming San Diego bands that she and Dex liked to listen to. She brushed her long blond hair back into her normal ponytail, then decided against it, letting it all fall loose around her face. She preferred it this way, actually, but Dex always told her that he liked her hair pulled back from her face, so she obliged, wanting to look good for him and not really caring all that much herself.

Tonight, though, she was feeling particularly rebellious—towards her mom and Chase, Dex and her whole life. She'd figure things out on her terms. All she had to do was hang in there and not get into any real trouble before she turned eighteen. That's when she felt like her life would really be starting. She'd felt that a lot over the past few years as things had gotten harder between her and her mom.

She carried her make-up bag into Andrea's small bathroom. She'd put on some mascara and a bit of blush—a meet-in-the-middle gesture for keeping her hair down—because she knew that Dex would appreciate that slightest bit of effort on her part.

Her eye caught the necklace that Kylie had given her right before she'd left. She'd tucked it into the clear zippered pocket of the make-up bag the night before when she'd been going through her purse looking for spare change. She felt tears stinging her eyes as she took it out of her bag and held it in the palm of her hand. She could still see the little girl's sweet smile when she'd given it to her, eyes all lit up as she waited for the reaction from Jemma that she knew would be quick to come.

Jemma placed the necklace around her neck, tucking it under her t-shirt. She'd always be Kylie's big sister—no matter what else happened. It was something that Jemma needed to make sure of.

She swiped her hand across her eyes and took once last look in the mirror, wiping the mascara away that now streaked across the top of her cheek. She took a deep breath and powdered her face before she walked back across the bedroom to pick up the shot of liquor that she was suddenly desperate for.

"You comin' out soon, babe?"

Jemma jumped, Dex's voice startling her as she turned toward the door.

"Dex. You scared me. Maybe try knocking next time."

"Noted. But I come bearing gifts." He grinned walking over to put his arm around her and hand her the shot he was carrying.

Jemma smiled as she took the alcohol from him, downing it in one gulp. "I guess I better catch up." She leaned in to give him a kiss on the cheek.

He turned his head to catch her lips with his own in a deep kiss, grabbing a handful of her loose hair and tugging it just a bit harder than she was comfortable with.

"Ow. Dex, stop."

He leaned his head back just a bit to look at her. "What's with the hair?"

"What? You don't like it?"

"You know I like it. I just prefer it when you wear it up off your face." He swatted her playfully on the behind.

Jemma took a quick mental assessment of his mood, deciding not to risk getting into an argument about something so stupid. She really wanted—needed—to have a good time tonight. She did love partying with Dex most of the time, when she was in the mood and drinking herself. That was her plan for this evening. To get drunk and forget all of her troubles for one more night. She'd make some decisions and figure out her next steps tomorrow.

She kissed him back on the lips and started walking towards the bathroom. "You go on. I'm gonna put my hair up—just the way you like it." She turned to blow him a kiss before he walked out of the room, yelling out for her to make it quick.

She pulled her hair back and stared at her reflection for what seemed like the hundredth time in the last few days. It was so surreal—to think that her whole life had been a lie. Who even was she now, and what could she count on to be true in her life?

She heard the notification sound of another text coming through and sighed as she walked across the room to turn off the volume on her phone. She was sure that it would be her mother but was surprised to see that it was a text from Gigi.

I'm worried about you, sweetie. Are you okay? Call me.

She wasn't surprised to hear from Gigi, but it was more surprising that Jemma had forgotten to get back to her earlier—and it was rare for her to do that to the woman whom she loved as if she were her grandmother—the only one she had now, she couldn't help adding in her head.

Jemma sent her a quick note back.

Sorry, Gi. I'm okay. Will call you soon. Please don't worry.

Another message came right back to her.

Of course I'm worried. I love you. Don't forget that and you be careful.

I know you do. I will and I love you too. xo

Jemma tucked her phone into her purse and stuck it in Andrea's closet. She wasn't going to think about calling anyone right now. She walked back over to the bedside table to have the second shot of alcohol that she'd not taken earlier when Dex walked in. It was good to feel the familiar burning in her throat for a few minutes. It was exactly what she needed, and as she walked out of the room into the loud music and laughter she could hear from the living room, she didn't want to have a care in the world. She was determined not to care about anything tonight.

CHAPTER 14

The party was in full swing when Jemma walked into the living room. Right away her eyes found Dex and Andrea, their heads close together on one of the sofas. When they leaned back, she could see that they were sharing a smoke, so her immediate bristle of jealousy relaxed just a bit. Andrea stood up quickly when she seemed to notice Jemma across the room—too quickly, Jemma thought as she crossed the room to sit down in the now available space next to Dex.

"What are you two doing all tucked away in the corner over here?" Jemma laughed as she kissed Dex on the cheek and tried to keep her mood light. But she didn't miss the quick look that passed between her boyfriend and Andrea. Was there something going on between them?

"Oh you know. Just getting into the party mood. Would you like some?" Andrea handed Jemma the joint that she and Dex had been smoking just seconds before.

Jemma took it and inhaled deeply. She needed to relax and this would help.

She was probably just imagining things about the two. Dex had never given her reason to think that he'd cheat on her. He had always seemed perfectly content with their relationship—if not a little bored. She couldn't help the thought that popped into her mind.

And there was the issue of the sex that she wasn't giving him. She looked at Andrea in her too-short skirt and the top that showed off her ample cleavage. For sure he could get what he needed from Andrea in that department. She knew she was judging, but she wasn't naive to think that Andrea would most likely have no problem letting Dex have what others paid for. If she trusted her gut, she could tell that there was an attraction between the two—one she probably needed to pay attention to tonight if she didn't want to lose her boyfriend.

Jemma leaned in closer to Dex, kissing him hard on the mouth and placing his hand on her thigh. He handed her the glass of clear liquid he was drinking from, and she didn't ask what it was before taking a big swig. She leaned back into the worn sofa as she felt the familiar burning in her throat and the almost instant lightheadedness that was a result of her current drink plus the two shots she'd had earlier. In general, it didn't take too much to get her feeling good, and she was well on her way to feeling no pain.

She looked around the room at the strangers that surrounded her, some laughing and seeming to be having a good time and some with eyes shut, seemingly tripping on something or other. From the looks of the back and forth involving one of the bedrooms, Jemma guessed there was more than just drinking and pot smoking going on at the party. She was beyond caring at this point, and way more interested in the drink Andrea was handing her than any sort of trouble she might be getting herself into. She needed to get rid of some of the heaviness that had been surrounding her the past few days. Tonight, she just wanted to be a normal seventeen-year-old, worry-free and intent on just having a good time.

She took a big drink from her glass, downing half of it and noticing Dex eyeing her with a big smile. His hand traveled up her thigh and she didn't resist as his mouth covered hers in a kiss that threatened to bruise her lips. She'd seen the look in his eyes. He was well beyond drunk and it wouldn't be long before he'd be passed out cold. Somehow the idea of this was appealing to her, and the irony of it as she let him kiss her so passionately did not go unnoticed, even as she let him stand up and lead her towards the hallway that led to the bedrooms.

She could fend him off. With all he had to drink—and God knows what else—tonight, she could easily persuade him of things other than sex. She pulled him toward her now in the narrow hallway, grinding her hips up against him and whispering in his ear. "Let's go in the kitchen. I want more to drink, okay?"

He let her pull him in that direction and then he

seemed to get a second wind, mixing her some kind of potent liquor concoction that had her sitting down the moment she'd tasted it. It crossed her mind for a second that she was going too fast—drinking too much—but she pushed her reasonable thoughts aside, reminding herself that she had one goal at that moment. She only wanted to get wasted and forget her problems for one more night.

CHAPTER 15

Jemma's throat felt raw and her head hurt beyond any hangover headache she'd ever had before. She tried to open her eyes, but everything was blurry. She caught a glimpse of all the white surrounding her and for a few seconds she wondered if she was dead—a thought that was both strange and amusing to her at the same time, because she didn't remember ever having any particular thoughts about heaven or any type of an afterlife.

She tried again to open her eyes, expecting to see Dex and any number of strangers passed out around her. She had a vague memory of Andrea's apartment—of accepting drink after drink from Dex and feeling a certain numbness as she downed one after another while sitting on that sofa with him. And possibly somewhere in her memory was the sound of a siren.

Her vision cleared and she could now make out her mom sitting beside her in a chair. Jemma was in a hospital bed and, feeling under the covers, she knew now that she was wearing a gown. She tried again to make her vision clearer. God, she was so thirsty.

"Mom," she managed, and her voice sounded beyond strange to her own ear.

Blu sat up quickly beside her and her hand went to Jemma's own, where Jemma could see the IV dripping something into her.

"Honey. How are you feeling?"

Jemma knew that look of worry on her mom's face and in that moment, she forgot all about the hurt and anger. She was scared. Really scared.

"Mom. Where am I? What happened?"

Blu was smoothing the hair back from her forehead—like she used to do when Jemma was a little girl. "You're in the hospital, honey. Do you remember anything?"

Jemma shook her head and grimaced at the pain it caused to do so. "Dex. Where's Dex?"

She saw her mom's lips tighten. She wasn't pleased at the mention of his name. That was for sure. How long had she herself been here? Long enough for her mom to get here from San Diego.

"I don't know where Dex is. I'm sure he's not particularly anxious to see me—after what happened to you."

"What did happen?" Jemma was confused. She couldn't remember any accident or anything related to why she might be here in the hospital with her mother.

Her mother eyed her carefully as Chase came into the room, walking over to place a gentle kiss on Jemma's forehead.

"You gave us quite a scare last night." He looked stern but Jemma could see the relief in his face.

"What happened?" She needed for someone to tell her what was going on. She guessed that it had something to do with the party, but she really couldn't remember anything beyond that. Good grief. Was she suffering from some kind of amnesia?

"Jemma, you had to be admitted to Emergency last night to have your stomach pumped." Chase said, putting his arm around Blu, who seemed to go a little pale at his words.

"Thank God, Dex—or whoever, at the place you were hanging out—had the sense to call 9-1-1. Jemma, you could have died," Blu said, her eyes filling with tears.

And Jemma believed what she was saying, even though the whole idea seemed a bit absurd to her.

Had she really had that much to drink? Had someone put something in her drink? She was feeling very confused when a doctor came in, a smile on his face, obviously pleased that she was awake and talking.

"So, young lady. How's your head feeling?" He bent close to her face, the fingers of one hand gently opening first one eye and then the other as he shone a bright light into each.

"Uhm. I've felt better." Among other things she was feeling, Jemma suddenly felt shy and embarrassed as the doctor helped her to a sitting position and proceeded to check her heart and her other vitals.

"Well, I bet you have." He winked at her and instantly Jemma felt more at ease. "I need to ask you some questions, Jemma." He turned to her mother and Chase. "Since she's under eighteen, I can't ask you to leave but I think it's to the benefit of Jemma that she feel unhindered in answering my questions honestly. My experience with minors is that she's more likely to do so with some privacy. But that is your decision."

He had a warm smile and Jemma decided that she did like him. Blu got up from her chair and leaned over to give Jemma a kiss on the forehead before taking Chase's hand.

"We'll just be out in the hall—if you need to talk to us after."

"Very good. Yes, I'll call you in when we're finished talking. Thank you." He pulled the chair over that Blu had been sitting in and stuck his hand out towards Jemma in one motion. "I'm Dr. Sanders, by the way. I was on call last night when they brought you in by ambulance."

"Nice to meet you, Doc." Jemma shook his hand, recognizing that her own handshake was less than firm. "So I came in by ambulance, huh? How strange."

"What's strange, Jemma?"

"It's strange that I don't really remember any of it."

"Well, you had a high degree of alcohol in your system—an amount that could have very well been fatal if your friends hadn't called for help."

"Really?" She didn't know if the slight disbelief she was feeling was the fact that she'd drunk enough alcohol to have her stomach pumped or the fact that any of those people at the party had had the sense to recognize that something was wrong with her.

"Yes, really." Dr. Sanders seemed to be studying her carefully and Jemma wondered if he had teenagers himself. He seemed to have a fatherly way about him. "Jemma, this is very serious. Do you understand that?"

She nodded her head slowly, wondering where he was going with the conversation. "How did my mom find out?" She didn't know yet how much the doctor knew about her situation—the fact that she was basically a runaway at this point.

"I guess one of your friends had the sense to give the paramedic your purse last night as they were loading you onto the ambulance. They got your mom's number from your phone inside." He was watching her face. "So really this conversation is about our discussing the alcohol poisoning—the seriousness of it. There'll be a social worker in later to discuss options for your treatment with your parents. The fact that you'd run away from home adds another layer to this puzzle that we're going to have to solve to be sure that you get the right help when you leave here."

Jemma had a knot in her stomach and a sense of foreboding like she'd not had before. "I'm almost eighteen." It was a whisper but Dr. Sanders heard her.

"Right. And until then, you're parents really do get to make the decisions about what is the best thing for you." He looked at her intently. "I've talked to your mom and I'm aware that you've been having some problems at home. Do you feel like this has had a big impact on your drinking?"

Jemma shook her head and then met the doctor's eyes. She was desperately trying to keep the tears from coming, but she knew she was failing as she felt the wetness on her face. "I dunno. I mean, I don't know if I drink more than other kids my age. And yeah, it's true that there's been a lot of stuff going on lately—bad stuff—that leaves me just wanting to forget everything, but I really don't think that I have a problem or anything like that."

Was he suggesting that she might be an alcoholic?

He was looking at her carefully again. "Jemma."

She nodded for him to continue, knowing it wasn't an argument that she'd be winning any time soon.

"Almost dying from alcohol poisoning is a problem."

She met his eyes, noticing again that they were kind, not judgmental. She nodded her head.

"It's a problem that we need to address. You're too young and you have too much ahead of you to be making mistakes that could cost you your life."

Jemma's tears were falling freely now. She didn't know if her crying was so much about the words he was saying to her or more because her time away with Dex in

LA was sure to be over now.

"I'm going to recommend to your mom that you go into a treatment center."

"Rehab?"

"Well, if you want to call it that, yes. But it's a different sort of program than what you are probably thinking about—one aimed at young people, like yourself."

"For how long?" Jemma could feel her guard—her defenses—going back up now. She was not going to a rehab program.

"Well. It's always a case-by-case basis, but typically you'd start with a minimum of thirty days—"

"I'll be eighteen in three weeks." Jemma interrupted him.

"Okay. It's true that when you turn eighteen, you'll be able to check yourself out—assuming that you aren't a threat to yourself any longer—but how about if we cross that bridge when we come to it?"

"Have you already discussed this with my mother?" A thought suddenly occurred to her. "She's not my mother, you know?" She watched his face for a sign of surprise. "Did you know that? I mean surely it's questionable what kind of decisions she is able to make for me at all."

"Linda is here too. I've met them both and they did fill me in on the larger points of the issues you've been having." He reached out to place his hand on Jemma's arm and she didn't move it away. "It's obvious to me that you have a family here that loves you and wants what's best for you. I'd like for you to remain in the hospital tonight—we need to get some more fluids in you. A social worker will be in later to discuss what needs to be decided before you leave, but for now, I want you to have a good long think about everything, okay?"

Jemma nodded and Dr. Sanders got up to leave, turning before he walked out the door. "I'll send your mother in now."

CHAPTER 16

Jemma felt stunned. How had she let things get so out-of-hand? She was still reeling from the fact that she was lying in a hospital bed. She thought about everything the doctor had just told her. She would not be going to rehab. She was pretty sure that she could talk her mom out of that idea—but Chase? That was another story. He'd have something to say about it, and he could be very persuasive with Blu when it came to Jemma.

Jemma's attention turned towards the door as it flung open.

She barely had a moment of recognition before Gigi was in the room and by her side, leaning down to give her a big hug and kiss.

"Oh, I'm so mad at you, darling girl. You gave us such a scare."

Jemma could see the tears in Gigi's eyes and her heart plummeted because of it.

"Gigi, what are you doing here?" In order for Gigi to have arrived from Guatemala, she would have had to have jumped on a flight late last night or early this morning. "Honestly, I'm going to be fine." She couldn't believe that her mom would have told Gigi to come all this way, but if she was being honest with herself, it felt wonderful that she was there—like somehow Gigi was going to help them all make sense of everything. She'd always been that for Jemma—a life raft of sorts during the stormiest of times with her mother and Chase.

"Yes, you are going to be fine, my lovely girl, and I've been thinking of coming anyway—ever since you seemed to have lost your mind just a little bit."

Gigi was teasing her, and Jemma laughed lightly as the older woman stroked her hair. Blu had slipped in and was quietly standing behind Gigi's chair.

"I think we've all lost our minds just a little bit," Blu said, also laughing lightly. She looked at Jemma. "Chase and Mom—Grandma—are down the hall—with Kylie."

"Kylie's here too?" For some reason Jemma hadn't stopped to think that her sister probably would be there. She was desperate to see her but she also didn't want to scare her. "Is she okay? About everything here, I mean?" Jemma asked Blu.

"Yeah, well, she was as scared as we all were when we arrived last night, but we've told her that you're going to be alright—that she can see you soon."

"Can I see her now?"

"Sure. You spend a little time with Gigi and I'll go get her."

Jemma reached for the necklace that no longer seemed to be around her neck. She motioned to the nurse who was placing fresh water next to the other side of her bed.

"Excuse me. I was wearing a necklace last night. Do you know where it is?"

The nurse nodded her head and opened a drawer in the table next to Jemma's bed. "All of your personal items are here."

Jemma reached over to grab the necklace, noticing that the delicate band had been cut, rather than released with the clasp.

"I know. Sorry about that. It's just protocol. They get a little scissors-happy in the emergency room sometimes—getting clothes and whatnot off the patients."

Jemma frowned but at least she still had the necklace. She noticed Gigi watching her, a question on her face.

"It's just something Kylie made for me right before— right before I left."

Gigi was staring at her intently. "You and your sister really do have a very special bond. Kylie looks up to you, you know, Jemma. And that's a responsibility."

"I know. And I know that she probably shouldn't— look up to me, I mean. I'm not the world's best role model as a big sister."

"Well, ya know what?"

"What?"

"You're all she's got."

Jemma looked at her, wondering what exactly Gigi was getting at.

"As a big sister, I mean. It's not like she's gonna get another one."

"I know." Jemma did feel bad when it came to Kylie.

"But let's talk about something else before she gets here."

Jemma looked Gigi in the eyes.

"What's your plan, Jemma? You're obviously not a child any longer, and you're getting close to having to make some pretty big decisions in your life."

Jemma looked down at her hands, too nervous to look Gigi in the eye. "About the money, ya mean?"

"Well, yes. But not just the money, honey. You have your whole future ahead of you and enough money to fund whatever education goals—or other *positive* endeavors—that you see in your future. I mean, have you even been thinking about any of that?"

"Kinda. I mean, I guess if I'm being honest, I probably got a little sidetracked this year."

Gigi had a funny look on her face as she leaned over and lightly pulled a strand of Jemma's hair. "Ya think, kiddo?"

Jemma laughed despite the sudden discomfort about the serious topic. Gigi had a way of doing that with her—getting her to think about serious things but in a way that wasn't quite so serious. Jemma loved that about her.

"Okay, I guess you have a point."

"Well, listen. Kylie's gonna be here soon and I'm sure Linda wants to see you. Afterwards, your mom and I are going to have some serious things to discuss with you, okay?"

"Like?" Jemma thought about what Dr. Sanders had said to her with his rehab recommendation, and she knew it would be a conversation to dread.

"Like, we'll talk about it in a little while."

They both looked up as Kylie came running into the room full-speed for Jemma's bed. The little girl climbed up and, after staring at Jemma for what seemed longer than the mere seconds it probably was, wrapped her skinny arms around her sister and squeezed her tight.

"I'm so glad you're okay, Jemma." Kylie's voice was muffled by the blanket that her face was nuzzled into. "I was so scared."

Jemma put her fingers under the little girl's chin, lifting her face so that they were looking at each other in the eye. "I'm really sorry, Kylie. And I'm okay. You know that, right?"

Kylie nodded her head and just hugged Jemma tight again.

Jemma looked over at her grandma, mom and Chase, not missing the tears coming down Linda's face. Jemma still could only think of her as her grandmother, but it did suddenly hit her again that Linda was her mother. She couldn't think about all that right now, though.

Her grandmother reached over Kylie to give her a kiss and hug, and Gigi stood up from the chair where she was sitting to give them all some more room. Jemma thought she saw a look pass between all of the adults in the room—for sure between her mom and Gigi—but she tried not to think about what was up with them as she focused her attention back on her sister lying in the hospital bed next to her.

"Are you going to come home with us?"

Jemma held her breath—not at all sure how to answer Kylie as she looked over at her mom and Chase. No, she was pretty sure that she would not be going home with them when she left the hospital.

"Kylie, we still need to figure all of that out." Blu had jumped in, saving Jemma from wondering what to say to her sister.

"Well, I don't want you to be gone any more." Kylie started to cry, and Jemma was quick to hug her close.

"Kylie, don't cry. Everything's going to be fine."

But in Jemma's head, everything was far from fine and she didn't know how to make sense of any of it.

Linda crossed the room then to gently pry Kylie away from Jemma's bed. "Come on, Kylie, let's go down to get that ice cream you've been wanting."

Kylie looked at Jemma as if for permission.

"Go on. That sounds good. Maybe bring me back an ice cream sandwich."

"Okay." Kylie gave her a last squeeze and then

followed her grandmother out of the room.

Gigi sat next to Jemma's bed with Blu and Chase right beside her. Jemma got the distinct impression that they were the united front and she should prepare herself for battle. But she had a feeling, even as she had the thought, that it was a battle she'd not be winning. She took a deep breath.

"Okay, so what is it? Why are you all looking at me like that? If it matters, I'm really sorry that I'm here—that we're all here—and that I've put you all through this. I really didn't mean for it to happen."

Chase reached over to put his hand on her arm. "We know that you didn't intentionally hurt yourself, Jemma."

Jemma nodded her head as Chase continued.

"But we're not willing to just sweep everything under the rug either. There's too much at stake." Chase's arm was around Blu, who'd started to cry.

"Jemma, I couldn't bear to lose you. I won't lose you." Blu reached down to hug her.

"I think you guys are being just a little bit dramatic here." Jemma bit her lip, judging it better to just listen first. "So what are we talking about then? Going back to San Diego, I assume?"

Her mom and Chase looked at each other before Blu spoke.

"No. We're prepared to follow Dr. Sanders' advice, getting you into a treatment center nearby—"

"No! I won't go to rehab!" Jemma could feel the tears falling as she sat up straighter in bed.

"Or—" Gigi had reached out to grab her hand now. "You can come back to the orphanage with me."

Jemma looked from Gigi to her mom and Chase, not sure what to make of the conversation, but pretty sure that they were giving her an ultimatum.

"We think that staying with Gigi and Douglas might be good for you—being away from your friends and the other influences in your life right now. Maybe that's enough to stop this pattern of drinking and partying. If it's not—and you really do have a problem with alcohol—then we can find you a treatment center—"

"—But I'll be eighteen then. You can't make me go once I'm eighteen." Jemma interrupted her mom.

"Yes, that's true." Gigi was squeezing her hand as she spoke to her. "I guess we're counting on you to really do some soul-searching to figure out what it is that you want for your life, honey. Sometimes it's easier to do that when you're able to get away from normal routine—from your normal life—which we all know hasn't been easy for you lately."

"So basically, the choice is up to you." Chase said. "You can either leave here to go straight into a treatment center or you can be on the plane to Guatemala with Gigi the day after tomorrow."

Jemma was crying. She didn't want to do either of those things. What she wanted was to see Dex—to just pretend that none of this was happening.

"Can I see Dex before I leave?" She was asking her mom.

Blu looked at Chase, who was nodding. "Can we trust you not to run away? Maybe we could all meet with him together."

Jemma cringed at Chase's suggestion. She didn't have a lot of options, though. She realized that. Only three weeks. She'd manage, and hopefully Dex would wait for her while she was gone.

"Okay." She leaned over to hug Gigi. "I'll go with you back to the orphanage."

Gigi reached out to push the hair back from Jemma's forehead. "Good. We'll have a great time. You'll see. And things will be better before you know it."

PAULA KAY

CHAPTER 17

As soon as the flight attendant made the announcement that they were free to move about the cabin, Jemma leaned her chair all the way back as she stared out the window. She angled her face and body even more, hoping that Gigi would think she was going to sleep. She wasn't ready to talk yet—not even to Gigi.

She closed her eyes as a few tears made their way down her cheeks, not bothering to wipe them away. She was remembering the conversation that she'd had with Dex the day before, after she'd gotten released from the hospital and they'd all checked into a hotel nearby.

When he had finally shown up after a lot of begging from Jemma, he'd been so cold to her. They'd had a quiet moment alone in the lobby—her mom and Chase nearby—and Dex had basically wished her well and told her that maybe they'd see each other if and when she returned to LA. One of Andrea's roommates was moving out and Dex had decided that he was going to continue living there.

Dex hadn't said it, but in her heart Jemma knew that

something had happened or was happening between him and Andrea. She knew that she should be angry about his lame half-breakup with her, but right now all she could feel was sadness. For all Gigi's talk about Jemma coming to the orphanage to do some soul-searching and figure out her future, Jemma had no idea what her future looked like, especially now that it was obviously going to be a future without Dex.

Her mom and Chase had been angry at the way Dex had just left Jemma crying in the hotel lobby. She couldn't help but smile, though, as she remembered the chat she'd had with Chase. He was always so quick to tell her that she deserved a wonderful man in her life, that she should never settle for anything less than someone who cherished and respected her—and he'd been quick to point out that Dex was not that young man.

Chase's words and her mom's hugs had made her feel better at the time, but now she just felt depressed again and there was still the weirdness between her and her mom and grandma. She just wanted it to all go away—for everything to be normal again.

She wiped the tears from her face, sneaking a quick look at Gigi sitting beside her. Gigi had been watching her and reached out to grab Jemma's hand in hers, which Jemma didn't resist. She always felt only love from Gigi— even when she was reprimanding Jemma, which she had been known to do.

"It's going to be okay, honey. You'll see."

Jemma nodded. "I know. And I know I haven't been the nicest person to be around the last few days, but I do appreciate what you and Douglas are doing for me— giving me another option besides the rehab, I mean."

Gigi was looking at her intently. "I don't really think you need rehab. And for the record, if I thought that's what you needed, I wouldn't have agreed to this."

"I know."

"Because the only thing that matters to me is that you're okay. Second after that is that I'm hoping spending a little time away from your friends, your mom—from your normal life, I suppose—will help you to get some clarity about your future."

Jemma looked over at her as she continued.

"We all need that sometimes, you know. Perspective. I know I can sure remember a time in my life—after Arianna had passed away for sure, but then also before Douglas and I went to Guatemala—that I really didn't know what was going to happen to make me feel better. It was a rough patch for sure."

Jemma vaguely did remember that time and hearing her mom and Gigi talk about the fact that Gigi had been feeling bad. Jemma knew that the orphanage had changed Gigi, and she also had fond memories of being there herself. Even though it really wasn't her ideal situation, it was certainly better than some rehab program, and maybe Gigi did have a point about getting away from everything.

Jemma sighed. Time would tell. She'd try her best to

put aside her misgivings and give it a chance.

She smiled at Gigi and then put her head on her shoulder, suddenly tired and wanting a little sleep.

Gigi squeezed her hand before letting it go. "I love you, Jemma. You just remember that."

"I love you too, Gi."

Jemma was tired and the motion of the small boat was making her even more sleepy. The trip to the orphanage was a longer one than she remembered. Once they'd landed in Guatemala City, there was the minivan ride to the river, which took several hours, but now they were in the last stretch of thirty minutes or so by small boat.

Jemma felt her face go a bit warm when she caught their boat driver looking at her. Gigi had told Jemma that Eduardo was one of about three drivers that they used to ferry them to and from the orphanage whenever they needed something from the small village nearby. She'd also whispered into Jemma's ear that he wasn't her preferred driver—that there were rumors about him having quite a reputation with the locals. Jemma didn't know exactly what that meant, but she was too tired to ask for clarification. It hadn't gone unnoticed by her that Eduardo had held her hand just a second or two longer than necessary when he'd helped the two women into the boat, and she couldn't help but wonder if Eduardo might add a little bit of excitement to her time there.

She smiled at him and when she saw that Gigi had her eyes closed, she moved up one seat so that she was nearer to where he was steering the boat.

"So is there anything fun to do around here?"

He eyed her carefully as he pulled a pack of cigarettes out of his jacket pocket.

"There's plenty fun to do here." He held the cigarettes out towards her.

After looking behind her at Gigi to see if she was still having a rest, Jemma took a cigarette out, inhaling as Eduardo lit it for her. She'd needed a smoke after the long plane ride and she knew that Gigi hated smoking, so she hadn't yet had the opportunity to sneak away for one.

She closed her eyes, feeling the effects of the smoke in her lungs. She really should think about quitting while she was here—she knew it was a horrible habit.

"If you know the right people to hang out with."

She opened her eyes, realizing that she'd totally spaced for a moment while Eduardo was talking.

"Sorry. I guess I'm more tired than I realized. What were you saying?"

The way he was looking at her was slightly unnerving, but mostly it just made her feel shy.

"I was just saying that I'm your guy, if you want any fun around here."

"Meaning?"

"Meaning, I know where to take you." He took a

slow drag from his cigarette and Jemma thought he looked extremely sexy.

"Is that right?" She took a puff of her own cigarette and spoke her words a bit softer as she noticed Gigi stirring a bit. "Why is your English so good?"

"Do you think so? Thank you." He gave her a wide smile, obviously pleased with her compliment.

"Yes. It is. Did you learn at college?"

Eduardo laughed and gave her a funny look. "Do I look like someone who would go to college?"

Jemma felt her face go warm again. He was teasing her and she wasn't quite sure how to handle it, but she did like the flirtation that seemed to be going on between them. It was definitely adding some possible excitement to what she'd been thinking would be a pretty dull three weeks in Guatemala.

"Well, I don't know if you've gone to college."

"Nah. School wasn't really my thing."

"Okay." She looked at him just as intently as he was looking at her. She could play this game too. "So what is your thing then?"

He smiled—maybe just a little too widely—and Jemma knew in that instant that Eduardo was trouble. But did she care?

"Wouldn't you like to know?"

She stared at him and shrugged. It was time to pretend that she didn't care what he had to say. She made a motion to move back towards where Gigi was sitting in the boat.

"I have a cousin who lives in New York—in the city. I lived with him for a year. So I suppose that's where I really learned English."

Jemma wondered what else he'd learned on the streets of the big city. She sat back down where she'd been sitting near him, but also did notice that Gigi seemed to be stirring a bit more. She took a last long drag of her cigarette.

"Jemma." Gigi's voice was sharp and it startled Jemma as she dropped the cigarette into the water, knowing that Gigi had already seen it; but it was a conversation they'd probably be having soon enough anyway.

She mouthed the word "later" to Eduardo and turned to make her way back to where Gigi was sitting.

"Sorry. I know you're not a kid, but it really bothers me to see you smoking." She laughed lightly. "And getting friendly with him."

Jemma felt like a child who'd been reprimanded but, oddly, with Gigi it never really seemed to bother her all that much. For some reason that she could never really explain, Jemma just really hated feeling disappointment from Gigi and Douglas. It had been that way for as long as she could remember.

"I know. I think I should maybe try to quit while I'm here." She eyed Gigi carefully.

"How about that you don't try as much as do quit.

It's a bad habit and one that won't be doing you any favors later in life." She reached out to put her arm around her. "I just want you to be healthy and happy. That's all. You know that, right?"

Jemma nodded, giving Gigi a hug. "I do know that. And I will try. I promise." She smiled, hoping it was enough to please her.

"And Jemma."

Jemma met her eyes.

"I'm serious about Eduardo." Gigi's voice was low so that he couldn't hear them talking from the other end of the boat. "He's bad news and I don't want you to get involved with him, okay?"

Jemma nodded but she wasn't quite ready to promise anything when it came to Eduardo. She could be sneaky, and if she had to sneak around a bit at the orphanage to have a little fun, so be it.

CHAPTER 18

Jemma noticed Rafael before he seemed to notice her as they pulled up to the dock at Casa de los Niños. She had to laugh at all of the kids jumping up and down screaming their hellos at "Mama Gi." She'd glanced at Gigi as they rounded the bend in the river and there was no mistaking the way that her whole face lit up when she saw the children. Jemma knew that the orphanage had become a treasured home to her and Douglas now—filled with the many children that they'd never had.

She glanced again at Rafael, making his way toward the dock with Douglas. He was so much taller than Jemma remembered—but he'd only been fifteen the last time they'd seen one another—both of them still children who'd become fast friends the summer that Jemma had been there. She wasn't sure why she hadn't thought much about him earlier, but now the memories of their easy friendship came flooding back to her.

"I've missed you so much." Douglas was helping Gigi out of the boat and winking at Jemma as he did so.

She watched the two embrace and share a deep kiss on the dock as the children swarmed around Gigi, all wanting their share of the hugs and kisses that they seemed confident would be doled out by the woman they called their mother.

While Gigi seemed distracted, Jemma took the opportunity to pass her number to Eduardo. She'd written it down quickly on a small piece of paper with a simple note that said that he should text her when he was coming back over in the boat. Eduardo held onto her hand for an extra second as he took the paper from her, and when he released her hand and she looked up, her eyes locked with those of Rafael, who was lifting the luggage out of the boat.

Jemma swore that she saw something flash across Rafael's face before he quickly looked away as if embarrassed by what he'd seen. She felt her stomach plunge—partly because she didn't want any awkwardness between herself and the boy who'd once been her best friend for an entire summer, but also because Rafael no longer looked like the boy she remembered. Rafael was tall, dark, and handsome.

"Jemma. It's so good to see you." Douglas had arrived by her side and she turned to give him a big hug.

"It's good to see you too. Thank you for having me."

"Well, you gave us quite a scare, you know." He squeezed her tighter and then pulled away to look her in the eye. "I'm expecting that you and I can have a nice chat about all of that at some point soon."

Jemma looked away, unsure of how to answer him. Rafael was still nearby—near enough that she knew he could hear their conversation—and she wondered what he knew about her being there. She turned her attention back to Douglas, who seemed to be waiting for a response.

"Yes. I know. I'm sorry about all of that. But I'm okay now." She met his eyes again, putting on a big smile. "Really."

Rafael had collected the two suitcases from the boat and was now standing politely beside Douglas. Douglas turned to put his hand on Rafael's shoulder and Jemma felt a bit shy all of a sudden.

"Jemma, you remember Rafael."

Rafael smiled at her and stuck out his hand.

She took it and then laughed as she pulled him in for a hug. He seemed surprised—she could feel it in his body—but then all of a sudden she felt him relax against her, squeezing her tighter.

They separated and Rafael took a step back. "You grew up."

"I did." She smiled at him, happy that their initial banter felt easy. "As did you."

He smiled back and picked up the suitcases. "Come on. I'll take you to your room."

Douglas had gone on ahead with Gigi and the kids—probably to give Jemma and Rafael a few minutes together. Jemma was tired and ready for a little nap before dinner, but she had to admit to herself that it did feel good being back. And as she walked beside Rafael to her room, she realized how much she wanted them to be friends again. She could use some new friends in her life. Gigi had insinuated as much to her on the plane, and Jemma wondered now if Gigi had had Rafael in mind when she'd made the statement.

Everything looked pretty much the same to Jemma since she'd been to the orphanage three years ago. Shortly after Silvia's death—when Gigi and Douglas had taken over at the orphanage—they'd had all of the buildings redone. They still retained a rustic charm, but modern plumbing had been installed and many other such things that made the living quarters much more comfortable for the kids, the volunteers, and the guests that had been coming more and more frequently over the years. When Jemma had visited over the summer, Gigi had put her in the dormitory with the older girls that lived here. The building that she and Rafael were standing in front of now was new. She was sure of it as she followed him up the steps to the small porch.

"They had this built for a few of us that are still here—after our studies have finished." He looked shy all of a sudden as he walked down a short hallway with Jemma's suitcase. "Well, actually it's just me right now, so you'll have plenty of privacy."

Jemma thought it was sweet for Rafael to be

concerned about her privacy. She also thought it interesting that Gigi and Douglas were putting them in the same house together. They must trust her more than she gave them credit for—or maybe they thought that Rafael was going to be a good influence on her.

Rafael had opened the door to a small bedroom with its own bathroom and little sitting area.

"I'm just down the hall on the opposite side and we share the kitchen and living room in that center area. I'll show you that now if you like."

Jemma nodded. She had forgotten how genuinely sweet Rafael was—so much Dex's opposite. The thought appeared before she'd even realized it. She sighed and Rafael looked at her.

"Sure. Thanks for helping me with my suitcase."

He nodded and motioned for her to follow him back out into the hall.

The rest of the house was simple but functional. There were four bedrooms in total and a nice-sized kitchen and living room area in the center. Jemma thought she'd feel right at home there—for a few weeks anyway. She was also pleased that it was a little bit set apart from where Gigi and Douglas stayed. She still had the idea in her head that there might possibly be a late-night meeting with Eduardo at some point. But she'd better not think about that just yet. She didn't want to risk anything bad happening with Gigi and Douglas before she'd had a chance to feel the situation out a bit.

Rafael was putting a tea kettle on the stove.

"Can I make you a cup of tea?"

In what universe was Jemma living in where a guy her age was actually offering to make her anything, let alone a cup of tea? She tried to pretend that she was answering a perfectly normal question. "Sure, thank you." She took a seat opposite Rafael at the small kitchen table as they waited for the tea kettle to whistle.

Rafael seemed to be looking at her carefully, and Jemma couldn't help but wonder what he was thinking.

Finally she spoke. *Just pull off the band-aid.* "So go ahead."

Rafael looked at her. "Go ahead, what?"

"I'm not sure if Douglas told you anything about why I'm here right now, but I've just been having a little bit of a hard time lately."

Rafael stood up to pour the hot water into the cups that he'd readied with the tea bags, and when he handed Jemma hers, she was surprised at what she felt when their fingers touched for a few seconds. She hadn't ever remembered feeling attracted to Rafael when she was fifteen. But then again, she'd thought very little about boys back then and now—now Rafael was not a boy. He seemed every bit a man, and so far, he seemed unlike any guy that Jemma had known.

Rafael was looking at her intently. "Well, I was with them when they got the call—from your mother." He reached out to touch her hand and she nearly jumped out of her chair at the surprise of his touch. "Jemma. I'm really glad that you're okay." He smiled at her. "I'm glad that you're here."

Jemma stood up from her chair. She felt her eyes burning and she didn't know if it was because she was so tired or if her emotions were about to burst forth in some embarrassing way in front of this handsome man. She did know that she needed a little time to herself.

"I'm glad I'm here too. It's nice to see you again, Rafael." She reached over to give him a slight hug. "Now if you'll excuse me—I think I need to have a little nap before dinner. See you at the dining hall later?"

"It's a date."

Jemma felt herself smiling as she walked down the hall towards her room, already feeling more herself than she'd felt in a very long time.

CHAPTER 19

Jemma walked into the dining hall feeling hungry and anxious to see some of the kids that she'd known years ago. Gigi and Douglas had left the basic structure of the building when they'd had it redone, so it was still open to the outside. She smiled when she saw Gigi walking toward her.

"How are you feeling, honey? Did you have a rest?"

"I did. Yes. Did you?"

"No." Gigi laughed. "Not really. Too much going on, and Douglas wouldn't leave me alone." She winked at Jemma.

Jemma laughed. "Okay. Say no more. I'm still a child, remember."

"Silly. I meant that he had lots to talk about."

"Sure. Sure you did."

Jemma was enjoying their light-hearted banter. Already things felt easier here. As she'd been getting ready for dinner, she'd taken a shower and just let her hair dry naturally, falling around her face the way that she liked. And no make-up—somehow being in the middle of the jungle with a made-up face just felt all wrong. She felt a sense of freedom after being there only hours.

"I think Rafael has a place saved for you." Gigi gestured towards one of the tables in the corner where Rafael sat taking to a little girl that Jemma thought she recognized as Maria. "Do you like your room, bella?" Jemma grinned. She'd not heard the familiar term of endearment from Gigi in a while and it reminded her of many good conversations that the two of them had shared over the years.

"I love the new building. And thanks for giving me a little space."

"Well, I know that you're not a child—that you might appreciate a little privacy." She seemed to be choosing her words carefully. "Douglas and I trust you."

Jemma leaned in to give her a hug. "Thank you. I appreciate that."

"Good. Now go over there and see what Rafael has on those plates for you."

Jemma made her way over to where Rafael was waiting for her, plates piled high with some type of chicken dish.

"Hi." His grin was wide. "Did you have a nice rest?"

"I did, thanks." Jemma walked around the table to sit down beside the little girl. "Are you Maria?"

She noticed the pad and pencil off to the side, beside Maria's plate.

The little girl nodded, her eyes wide. "Do you

remember me?"

"I do. Yes." Jemma smiled widely at her. "Can I sit by you?"

"Yes." Maria smiled back and slid over on the bench just a little. "I wanted to say hi to you, and Rafael said that you wouldn't mind."

"I don't mind at all." Jemma pulled her legs over the bench and sat down to dig into her food. "Is that your drawing?" She gestured toward the paper beside the little girl.

Maria nodded, a big smile on her face. "Yes, I was just trying to draw a portrait of Rafael." She giggled as he wiggled his eyebrows at her across the table. "But he never sits still long enough for me."

"Your drawing is quite good."

"Do you like to draw?" Maria asked her.

"I used to." Jemma smiled at her. "You must be about seven now? Is that right?"

"Yes. I'm turning eight next month."

Jemma felt a pang in her stomach. She really must call Kylie soon. Sitting here with Maria now reminded her of her sister, and she wanted to be sure to stay in touch with her. Her hand automatically went to the necklace around her neck. Somehow in the day before they'd left LA, Gigi had managed to take it somewhere and get it fixed for her. She noticed Maria and Rafael both watching her.

"Shall we?"

Rafael nodded as the three ate their meal in silence

for a few minutes, Jemma content to look around the busy room, memories flooding her about the last time she'd been here. She waved to Tori, who was sitting across the room with a table full of kids. Tori had been the first person to introduce Gigi and Douglas to Casa de los Niños all those years ago. She'd been at the orphanage for ten years and Jemma doubted that she'd ever leave.

"Maria is being adopted." Rafael's words broke into Jemma's thoughts.

Jemma looked down at the little girl beside her, who had a big smile on her face.

"Are you?"

Maria nodded. "Yes. My mother and father are coming to pick me up soon. I'm going to live in America."

Jemma met Rafael's eyes across the table. She knew that it was unusual for the kids here to be adopted these days. Most of them would spend their entire childhoods at the orphanage and then go on to college or move to the city to find jobs—or stay on and work at the orphanage as Rafael had apparently done.

"Are you excited about moving to America?" Jemma asked the little girl, curious to know her answer.

"I'm excited to have parents." She grinned and Jemma felt her heart beat a little faster.

"I bet your parents are very excited about getting you also."

"Do you think so?" Maria asked the question like she

was genuinely unsure.

"Maria." Rafael voice was quiet.

"Yeah, Raf?"

"They're just as excited as you are." He smiled at the little girl. "And what are we gonna do without you around here?" He winked at her and Maria laughed.

"I don't know. I guess you'll have to find someone else to make you my famous dessert."

Jemma thought the whole exchange between the two was quite endearing. She looked down at Maria. "What's your famous dessert?"

Maria laughed. "Oh, it's just this lime pie. Fernanda taught me how to make it last year and it's Raf's favorite."

"Maria. It is not *just* a lime pie." Rafael feigned a look of shock and then directed towards Jemma. "It's *the* best lime pie you'll ever taste."

Jemma laughed at the two and looked over again at Maria, who was giggling and looking up at Jemma.

"It is pretty good. I'll make it for you sometime— before I leave."

"That would be great. I love lime pie." Jemma smiled and put her arm lightly around the young girl's shoulders to draw her in for a little side hug.

The three finished their meal and then Maria got up to start collecting their plates.

"Thank you," said Jemma. "You don't have to do that."

"I do, actually. It's my job."

Jemma caught Rafael's eye and remembered the tight ship that Gigi, Douglas, and Tori ran here. Everyone had their chores and everyone worked together—and played together. Silvia had always seen to that when she was alive, and it was something that Gigi and Douglas had kept going when they took over.

Once Maria had left with their dishes, Jemma turned her attention to Rafael. "And you? What are you doing these days?"

"I'm mostly the resident handyman, I guess. But I'll do pretty much whatever Douglas needs around here. Usually it's fixing things or building something, but sometimes I'll go to meet someone in the city—a volunteer or guests to bring here. And I do also help out with the kids when we're short on volunteers—or when I'm bored, basically." He laughed. "What about you? What's going on in the world of sunshine and movie stars?"

Jemma remembered how funny she'd thought Rafael's perceptions of America were when she'd met him. It seemed like a lot of the people here had a strong impression of the United States based on whatever current popular TV series had made its way there. But she'd also had the big realization that her life at the beach in La Jolla actually was a little bit like those TV shows, so then she'd had to explain that she kind of knew that her life wasn't necessarily typical of that of a fifteen-year-old American girl. It had all been rather confusing to Rafael at the time. She had to stifle a laugh at just how much more confusing her life might seem right now.

"That's kind of a long story." She laughed.

"I'd like to hear it." His face was kind, his smile genuine. "Shall we go for a walk?"

Jemma got up from the table, smiling at him. "We shall."

She caught Gigi's eye from across the room. She and Douglas were sitting at a table laughing with a large group of kids. Gigi smiled and waved to her before Jemma turned to follow Rafael out toward the path that she remembered led through the jungle.

The two walked for a few minutes in silence, Jemma taking in the lushness of the trees and various plants that she remembered loving when she was here last. She used to bring a sketchpad out here and sketch various scenes for hours at a time. It had really been a very creative time for her now that she thought about it—a time unlike any she'd had since. She sighed, feeling the weight of everything that had happened since she'd last been there.

"Is something wrong?"

Jemma eyed Rafael carefully and gestured towards a big log off of the path. "Can we sit?"

Rafael nodded, taking off one of the two shirts he had on to lay it across the log before Jemma sat down.

Her heart melted just a bit more at the kind gesture and then she opened up to Rafael more than she'd opened up to anyone—maybe in her whole life—telling him everything until it seemed she had no more words to speak or tears to cry.

CHAPTER 20

Jemma relaxed fully into the embrace that Rafael had offered her when she'd finished speaking. Her tears were lessening and she felt emotionally drained but more comfortable with another person than she'd felt in a long time. She glanced up at Rafael and then slowly made herself sit up on the log next to him, eyeing him carefully.

His gaze was so intense, the concern so obvious on his face.

"Are you okay?"

Jemma nodded. "I think so. Sorry for dumping all that on you. Not really sure where that need came from all of a sudden." She laughed lightly, hoping to lighten the mood.

Rafael was quick to reach over and take her hand. "Don't feel like that. You can tell me anything. I mean that, Jemma."

She felt a stray tear slip down her face at the gentleness of his touch and his words. It had been so long since Jemma had trusted anyone—since she'd let her guard down so completely—that she still couldn't quite believe that she'd shared so much with him.

"Thank you. That really means a lot to me."

She'd told him everything she could think of—about the money, about Dex, about the partying and her running away and about what she was supposed to be doing and figuring out while she was here at the orphanage.

Rafael had listened so attentively, and even though their lives had been so different, she didn't feel any judgment from him at all.

"Do you want to talk more about it—about what your ideas are for the future?"

Jemma didn't want to talk anymore. She was very tired all of a sudden. She shook her head. "Ya know, I think I really need to get some good sleep. Do you mind if we head back?"

"No, not at all. It's a good idea, I think."

They walked back in silence. Jemma stopped off to say goodnight to Gigi and Douglas and also to have a quick chat with Tori, whom she'd not said hello to yet. She promised she'd see them all at breakfast and went back to her room to settle in for a good night's sleep.

As she drifted off, she couldn't help but have a few doubts about having shared so much with Rafael. Maybe it had been too much. She'd grown used to keeping her thoughts and her emotions to herself, so it felt odd and disconcerting that this man she barely knew anymore knew so much about her and her current problems. She had never opened up to Dex like that—at least not about her real feelings. She didn't know exactly what had made her do it, but she hoped that she'd have some clarity about it all in the morning when she woke up rested.

The rest of the week seemed to pass slowly to Jemma. She spent most of her time in her room listening to music or watching something on her laptop. She knew that she'd been avoiding Rafael ever since they'd...since she'd had the big talk with him—spewing every single thing that was ever bothering her out of her mouth. She'd had a lot of regret after that night, waking up that next morning convinced that she'd made a mistake to share so much of herself. She was embarrassed, and Rafael's attempts at trying to talk to her since then had only strengthened her resolve to keep to herself.

She was cordial when they happened to see one another in the kitchen or for meals in the dining hall, but she knew she was being standoffish and she didn't care. Gigi had been by to talk to her that morning, asking her what was wrong and trying to convince her to come join the others in some activities. And she'd also asked her about Rafael—if something had happened between the two of them.

Jemma had told her that everything was fine—that she just felt like being alone—to think about things, she had told Gigi, but she was pretty sure that Gigi wasn't buying it. Jemma was just marking off the days until she turned eighteen in two weeks. On her birthday, she'd buy a ticket to LA and hope that Dex would be there to pick her up on the other end. Well, she actually hadn't heard anything from Dex—her texts and e-mails had gone unanswered so far, but she still held out hope. If not, she'd figure everything out on her own once she got to LA.

She'd ask Douglas about accessing her trust—he was the trustee and she knew that he'd give her that information, so she'd be able to check into a nice hotel or do whatever she wanted when she returned to LA.

The ding from her phone of an incoming text interrupted her thoughts. She'd only really been texting with her mom, Chase, and her grandmother, who had been checking in with her daily. She was telling them everything was fine, but she was sure that they'd been speaking to Gigi also, so who knew if they really believed her? At least she was keeping out of trouble. That was the thing that would keep them all happy.

She looked down to see a text from a number she didn't recognize.

Hey beautiful.

She smiled.

Who is this?

She knew who it was. When Eduardo hadn't sent her anything the first few days after she'd met him, she assumed that he hadn't been interested in her after all. Now she was happy for the possibility of some excitement—or at least some flirtation.

Your secret admirer.

Jemma bit her lip as she thought about how to respond—how far to take it with Eduardo. She did seem to gravitate towards the "bad boys" for some reason. And she was a bit bored.

What if I don't want it to be a secret?

She hit the send button and felt her heart racing as she waited for his response.

Meet me at the dock tonight at midnight. I'll bring the beer, you wear something sexy.

She was playing with fire. And she didn't care.

I'll be there.

She could sneak out at midnight, no problem. She knew that it was pretty quiet at night, and as long as they didn't make a lot of loud noise they could hang out near the dock without anyone knowing.

She took a shower and got ready for dinner, careful to not display anything out of the ordinary. She'd change her clothes and put on just a touch of make-up later before she met Eduardo.

Jemma took her normal spot at the table in the corner with Maria, noticing Rafael watching her from across the room. She felt bad if she thought about him too much, so she pushed the thoughts aside; but it was always hard to be in the same room with him and not feel bad. She hadn't wanted to hurt him. That was for sure. She sighed. She really was a jerk.

Maria looked at her from across the table. "What's wrong?"

"Nothing, why?"

"You just made that loud sighing noise."

"I did?"

"You did."

Maria was grinning at her, and Jemma made a mental note to call Kylie the next day. She missed her sister terribly, and having gotten close to Maria was reminding her of that every day.

She finished her dinner, opting out of the pre-bedtime campfire ritual—just as she'd done every night since she'd been there—and she lay on her bed waiting for midnight to come. She'd changed into the one top she had that did reveal some cleavage and made up her face just the way that Dex had liked it. What was good enough for Dex would probably impress Eduardo.

At eleven fifty-five, she grabbed a small flashlight and quietly slipped out the door. It was dark outside but the light she carried shone just enough for her to make her way to where the swimming hole and dock were. As she got nearer she could make out a small light and figured out that it was the cigarette that Eduardo must be smoking. God, she was dying for a cigarette.

She walked over to where he stood, suddenly feeling a bit shy. She really hoped that she'd have enough instinct and good sense not to mess around with anyone too bad.

Before she could even think about what he was doing, Eduardo had pulled her close and was kissing her on the mouth. Though she was taken by surprise, she didn't resist. It felt good to be kissed—to be wanted in that way again. Still, she wondered if there was an underlying danger to the excitement she was feeling. She could feel the strength of his body against hers and she had the distinct impression that Eduardo was not someone to play with.

But she loved the excitement of it.

She pushed him away after an intense minute or two of kissing to look at his face in the moonlight.

"Wow. It's nice to see you too." She laughed, but Eduardo didn't look like he was into joking around.

He tried to pull her towards him for another kiss, but she held him at a distance, gesturing towards the cigarette that he still held in his hand. "Can I have a drag of that?"

He handed it to her, a smile on his lips. "You look delicious." He reached out, putting his hand just under the low neckline of her shirt, startling her as she felt his fingers on her breast.

She reached up to remove his hand with her free one, laughing more out of nervousness now.

"Easy there, tiger. Slow down."

He eyed her with a funny look, taking the cigarette back from her when she offered it.

Fire. That's what Eduardo was. She should know

better. The thoughts came from somewhere, so apparently she wasn't totally oblivious to possible danger. But did she care?

"Don't be a tease."

"I'm not a tease."

Just an idiot sometimes.

"I think you're teasing me." He was smiling, but she didn't know where he was going with the statements.

She took a step toward him, allowing him to pull her close again and feeling the length of his body up against her own. He put his hand at the back of her head, pulling gently on her hair as he kissed her hard again on the lips, his tongue strong and forceful in her mouth.

"Come with me." He'd taken her by the hand and was leading her to the boat.

"Where?"

"Some place a little more comfortable."

He kissed her again, and the shivers she felt weren't from the kisses. Something in the back of her mind restrained her. She wouldn't go with him. Not tonight.

"No, I can't. Not tonight."

"See. I told you."

"What?"

"You're a tease."

"I'm not, but—"

"But what?"

"You should know that I don't sleep around."

She wouldn't tell him that she was a virgin—way

inappropriate, and she had the feeling that it would only make him more interested.

"I don't want you to sleep around." He was smiling at her again. "I just want you to sleep with me—to be mine while you are here." He kissed her again, and again she removed his hand from her breast and then from her thigh.

"I gotta go."

She wanted to have some fun but she didn't want this—fighting off a guy she hardly knew who seemed to have a hard time when it came to the concept of hearing a girl say no. What she wanted was a party—to lose herself to a few drinks for an evening.

"Okay. How about tomorrow night? I'll take you to a party."

He let go of her and he seemed a little less intense.

"What kind of party?"

"A fun kind of party. You'll see. Pick you up at ten o'clock."

"I think ten is too early. I need to be sure everyone is asleep. Not before eleven thirty."

"Okay. Eleven thirty." He leaned over to kiss her, much more gently this time—almost sweet.

She smiled, her fears eased, as she kissed him back. Then she walked back to her place in the dark.

CHAPTER 21

Jemma opened the door quietly and slipped into the small foyer.

"Hey."

Her heart practically jumped out of her chest for being startled as she looked toward the kitchen, where Rafael's voice had come from.

"God, Rafael. You scared me."

"Sorry." He was eyeing her carefully as she made the few steps into the kitchen.

"What are you doing?" She was annoyed that he'd startled her and even more annoyed that he'd caught her sneaking back into the house.

"I'm getting a drink of water. What are you doing?"

She purposely looked him right in the eyes, daring him to say more than he should. "Nothing. I was just out getting some fresh air."

"Okay."

She knew he didn't believe her and she didn't care. It was none of his business. But she also didn't need him going to Gigi and Douglas about anything. She eyed him carefully. She doubted he'd rat her out, but she couldn't be sure.

She reached for a glass in the cupboard. Rafael took it from her, filling it with water before he gave it back to her. *Always the gentleman.*

"What, Rafael?" He looked like he wanted to say something, and Jemma would just as soon have it out right now so that she didn't have to think about having another run-in with him later about it.

"Well, I've never seen you with make-up on since you got here."

She just stared at him. He knew. She didn't really care.

"Well, I guess that's really none of your business, is it?"

She saw him flinch. Her words sounded harsher than she'd meant them.

"Jemma."

"What?"

She was daring him to continue.

"Be careful."

She glared at him.

"He's no good. He's not good for you."

Jemma felt her heart beating a little faster. It was Rafael. The way he was looking at her. She knew that he cared about her—and that she'd been such a jerk to him ever since that night. When they'd gotten so close—when she'd shared so much with him. Too much.

"Just mind your own business, okay? You don't know

what's good for me."

Jemma picked up her glass of water and turned to walk away.

"I just care about you, Jemma."

She pretended that she hadn't heard his quiet words as she walked down the hall to her bedroom.

She did a good job keeping to herself all day, just like she'd done pretty much every day since her arrival at the orphanage. She was a little surprised that Gigi and Douglas had left her alone as much as they had. She knew that they'd been very busy with things going on at the orphanage, but she would have thought that she'd have gotten a lecture or two by now. Aside from the short talk she'd had with Gigi the other morning, neither of them had pressed things with her. She had a feeling that it was coming, though—Douglas had tried on more than one occasion, but so far Jemma had managed to escape it with mention of a headache or something else that required her to spend time alone in her room.

Now, though, she'd asked Douglas if she could make a phone call from his office. It was the best place on the property to do anything that required an Internet connection, and she had been popping in there occasionally to catch up on e-mails and make phone calls. She'd done her best to avoid talking to her mom and grandma as much as possible, but she didn't want to do the same with Kylie. If that meant the occasional chat with the others, so be it.

She checked her e-mail while she waited for Douglas to leave the room, giving her the privacy that he'd promised. Nothing from Dex, as per normal. She sighed and noticed Douglas looking at her from behind his desk.

"Everything okay?"

"Yeah."

"Jemma, you know that you can talk to me, right? About anything, I mean."

"I know."

"I'm a good listener and I'll try very hard to understand where you're coming from."

Jemma gave him a smile. Douglas was one of the kindest men she knew. It was a little funny, really, if she thought about it. She kept choosing loser boyfriends, but she'd only had the best male role models in her life— Douglas and Chase. She *should* know better, and maybe one day she'd go to therapy like her mom was always suggesting to figure out what the heck was going on with her.

Douglas was now standing beside her and she let him hug her on his way out.

"I know. I promise I'll talk to you if there's anything going on with me."

When had she become such a good liar?

For now, she needed to focus on a phone call with Kylie, and that probably meant getting through her mother first. She took a deep breath and dialed the number.

Finally, it was time to meet Eduardo at the dock. Jemma thought the day would never end.

She'd had a hard time getting Kylie on the phone earlier. As predicted, her mom had wanted to talk; apparently she and Chase had had several conversations with Gigi who was, in fact, expressing concern about Jemma and how much time she'd been spending alone.

After convincing her mom that she was spending good time alone to really think about her life and where it was going, she was finally able to talk to Kylie for a few minutes before the younger girl had had to leave to go to one of her friend's birthday parties—most of the call had been spent with Kylie crying when Jemma had not been able to give her an answer as to when she'd be coming home.

Now, though, Jemma was just excited about the prospect of going to a party and having a few drinks. She knew when she'd first met Eduardo that if there were any fun to be had around there, he'd be the ticket. Even though he'd been a bit over-the-top last night, she knew that she could handle him—and besides, the idea of a night out sounded too good to pass up.

She carefully closed her bedroom door and made her way down the hall. She'd taken care to put on a bit more make-up tonight and she was wearing one of the casual cotton dresses she'd brought with her. She was feeling good and ready to party.

God. She could see that there was a light on in the kitchen—there was no way that she could get out of the front door without Rafael seeing her if he was in there. As she got closer, she could see that he was sitting at the table.

She stopped for a few seconds in the hallway. She was already running late and didn't know how long Eduardo would wait for her, so she'd just risk Rafael's knowing and count on the fact that he'd keep it to himself.

"Hey."

She tried to just keep walking past him.

"Hey yourself. Sneaking out again?"

"I won't be late. Don't wait up," she added, hoping it sounded as sarcastic as she meant it.

She heard Rafael getting up from the table as she opened the door to step out unto the porch.

Please don't follow me.

"Jemma."

She heard him calling out but pretended not to as she hurried down the path toward the dock. At least he'd not been shouting at her. She was thankful for that. He probably didn't want to get her in trouble. She didn't really doubt Rafael's motivations for being concerned for her. She had to be honest with herself about that.

She smiled as she saw the now familiar light of

Eduardo's cigarette as she walked out onto the dock.

He grabbed her in a hug, giving her a slight kiss compared to the ones she'd received from him last night. She was thankful for this, as it made her feel more at ease about leaving with him in the boat.

"Hi. I might be being followed, so we should go—as in quickly." She grinned, ready to get the party started as she caught a glimpse of the beer in Eduardo's boat.

"You're my kinda party girl, babe."

Eduardo threw his cigarette in the water and helped Jemma into the boat. Once she was settled, he opened up one of the beers, handing it to her.

"You go ahead and start on yours. I'm going to paddle until we're out just a bit before I start the engine. Come here." He motioned for her to lean forward, and she was definitely noticing how sexy he was in his jeans and black t-shirt, the moonlight catching that look in his eyes—the look that promised just a hint of danger.

Jemma obliged, leaning forward carefully to give him a full kiss on the lips. Tonight Eduardo seemed more in control of his desires. But she did still see that look on his face. She'd do her best to encourage his drinks along with her own, hoping that enough alcohol in his system would mellow him out when it came to any thoughts other than just having a good time together.

She leaned back now, watching him down a beer as she started in on her own, more than ready to get the party started.

PAULA KAY

CHAPTER 22

Jemma rested her head back against the sofa, allowing herself to feel the buzz after several beers and the last of two shots of tequila that Eduardo had talked her into. She opened her eyes, taking in the party around her. She laughed lightly because it could have been any party she'd been to back home—were it not for the Latin music playing and the fact that she was the only light-skinned girl around. It was all the same, really. A bunch of young people sitting around getting drunk, smoking, and every once in a while disappearing into some secret room in the back in which Jemma could take a good guess about what was happening. Either drugs or sex—or both, more likely.

Eduardo had been able to dock the boat at a place where they could then walk to his cousin's house. It was a small village, and he said that the party would be packed—that everyone from miles around knew about it. It was how things worked around there—also similar to back home, Jemma thought.

Jemma looked up as Eduardo sauntered back into the living room where she was sitting. He'd disappeared for nearly thirty minutes, and Jemma guessed he'd been to the back room for a little something extra himself. He'd not invited her to join him and she'd been content at the time to just sit and enjoy her beer, chatting with a few of the girls who seemed quite interested to learn more about her and what she was doing there.

Now Eduardo was back, and Jemma wasn't sure how she felt about the look in his eyes as he pulled her to her feet. He was definitely stoned, and the smile that was so sweet earlier now resembled more of a leer. She laughed, feeling a bit dizzy as she stood up. She'd lost track of how many drinks she'd had and now Eduardo was handing her another shot. A little voice inside her head—quite possibly the good doctor's—was telling her that one more might be too much, but she took it anyway. Last one and then she'd be feeling no pain.

Eduardo was kissing her now, pinning her up against the wall with his strong body. She didn't mind. His tongue felt good in her mouth, his touch exciting to her. She did notice a few of the girls whispering on the couch as they stared at her, and she did wonder for a moment what that was all about.

"So, do you make out with all the young American girls like this?" she whispered in his ear.

"Only the really cute ones." He lifted his mouth just enough to speak the words, and just as quickly she felt his deep kiss again as his hands found their way under her dress from where they'd started on her thigh.

She grabbed at his hand to stop him, laughing as she did so.

"No. We have an audience." She looked over at the women on the sofa and Rafael's head turned just a bit to see what she was looking at.

"So, you don't like an audience? I thought you might secretly be a naughty girl?"

He was laughing, being playful with her, and in her drunken state she was loving the flirtation.

She reached around his neck and pulled him to her for a kiss to which he obliged, letting out a slow moan inside her mouth. He pulled away to look at her and when he grabbed her hand to lead her down the hallway, she knew that she might be in trouble. But she didn't have the wits about her to care—or to do much about it once they reached the door to what appeared to be an occupied bedroom.

Eduardo said something to the guy in Spanish. He laughed and the woman he was with got up to grab her clothes by the side of the bed, shooting Jemma a look that was anything but pleasant.

As the two left the room, Eduardo grabbed her by the hand, pulling her down on top of him on the bed. Even with her foggy brain, Jemma knew that things were going too far, but she didn't have the strength or the desire to stop him—not yet, anyway.

In one quick motion, he'd flipped her over so that he was now on top of her, kissing her hard as his hand found its way up her skirt. She could feel how strong he was, and his kisses weren't playful or sexy anymore. She could feel the bruising of her lips, and her face felt sensitive where his whiskers were rubbing against her.

"Hey. Hey, Eduardo. Not so hard. You're hurting me."

He stopped to look at her, his hand slowing to a gentle rub of her thigh. He continued to stare at her intently, the stalled intensity confusing Jemma a little bit. He wasn't hurting her now but she knew the look that she saw in his eyes. She'd do well to get them out of the bedroom—even in her drunken state, she knew that much.

"Do you like that?" He was watching her face intently as his fingers found their way closer and closer to the elastic of her underwear.

He thought he was teasing her in a way that would turn her on, but inside she was starting to feel nervous, wondering if she could turn the situation around and get back to the living room where they could enjoy a few more drinks.

She gently placed her hand on his with some firmness, causing him to stop the motion of his fingers on her thigh, and he looked at her with a question on his face. "Eduardo, let's just kiss, okay?" She pulled him toward her so that his lips were on her own again. "I like your kisses—the gentle ones." She laughed, trying to keep things light.

"Oh, you're gonna get a lot more than kisses from me tonight." His mouth was rough against hers again, his hands pulling her underwear down, and she couldn't stop it. "I'm gonna give you what you came here for."

"Get off of me."

She was crying now, aware that things were going bad but not sure how she was going to be able to stop it. She saw the anger flash across his face and just as his hand was reaching for the button of his jeans, the door swung open.

Jemma tried to scramble out of the bed and adjust her clothes all at the same time as Rafael preceded to land a couple of good punches to Eduardo's face after he'd pulled him off Jemma.

"Rafael."

She didn't know what to say, but she had never been so grateful to see someone in all her life. She watched him land another punch square to Eduardo's eye before he muttered for Rafael to stop. Rafael brought his arm back and Jemma gently stopped him from taking another punch.

"Stop. That's enough."

Rafael looked at Eduardo, who was now cowering on the floor, his face bloodied, his drunken body curled up into a fetal position.

"Don't come near her again. Do you understand me?"

Jemma was slightly shocked at the intensity of

Rafael's rage. When he reached for her hand, she didn't resist and let him lead her through the house and out the front door toward the dock where she'd been only hours ago with Eduardo.

"Rafael, I—"

"Don't talk." He helped her into the small boat docked next to Eduardo's and she could see that he was still very angry.

She got in and sat down where he directed her, not saying a word as she watched him untie the boat and start the engine. As they sped away, she put her head in her hands as she leaned forward, suddenly feeling very ill.

"Raf—I-I'm gonna be sick. Can you stop the boat?" She was doing her best to be sick over the side even before he'd had a chance to cut the engine. Her body convulsed as the tequila had its way with her stomach. She felt Rafael's hands gently pulling her hair back as his arm went around her waist, helping her to lean further over the edge of the boat.

She sat up, knowing that her face was streaked with tears—and vomit.

Rafael's arm left its position from around her as he wrung out his shirt that he'd dipped into the river. He gently wiped her face with it and then put his hand under her chin to tilt her face up. He looked into her eyes.

"Are you okay, Jemma?"

She was still drunk but she recognized his genuine concern. She nodded her head and looked down at her hands in her lap. She was embarrassed—and grateful, extremely grateful.

"Did he hurt you? Tell me the truth."

Jemma shook her head. "No. You got there just in time—I'm sure of that. How did you know? Where I was, I mean?"

"I knew about the party—everyone knew around here. It didn't take a lot to figure out that it was where that lowlife would be taking you." He gently took the elastic band from her ponytail and used his shirt to wipe something—vomit, most likely—out of her hair. "Yeah, you got a little something in your hair." He laughed lightly as she scrunched up her nose. He winked at her and used his fingers to fan her hair out around her shoulders. "And by the way, I like your hair down like this."

She looked at him then and burst into tears, letting him pull her to him for the big hug that she'd probably been needing more than she realized.

"Shh." She felt his kiss on the top of her head as she nestled against his chest. "Everything's gonna be just fine." He pulled away after a few seconds. "Are you okay now? I'd like to get you home before daylight." He winked again and she was thankful that he wasn't mad at her when she knew he had every right to be.

She nodded her head and he moved back into position to steer the boat again.

PAULA KAY

CHAPTER 23

Jemma was trying to pay attention to Rafael's voice telling her that she needed to be quiet. She was having a hard time keeping on the path even though Rafael had a firm grip on her arm as he attempted to lead her back to where she could finally lie down to sleep. She was tired and still feeling quite drunk. She wasn't used to drinking tequila and it was more than what she could handle.

"Raf—I need to stop—"

She'd barely gotten off the path and into the bushes before she was heaving and feeling like she was going to die. Once again, Rafael held her hair back from her face and she could feel his hand on her back.

"Jemma. Shh. Try to be quiet."

"Why? I can't help—"

"It's Douglas. I can see him with a flashlight. Okay, he's coming this way. Are you done? Can you stand up and try to act normal?"

"What's going on over here?" Douglas was shining a flashlight towards them that made Jemma cover her eyes with her arm.

She wiped her mouth off with her hand and did a quick swipe under her eyes, hoping that her face looked somewhat normal.

"Rafael, is that you?"

Jemma was standing slightly behind Rafael and she knew it was just a matter of seconds before Douglas would be close enough to see them both. *Act normal. Pull yourself together.* She took a step so that she was standing beside Rafael, just as Douglas was close enough to see them on the path.

"Jemma? What are you two doing out here? It's three thirty in the morning."

Douglas was looking at her intently.

"Oh, I couldn't sleep." Jemma couldn't tell if her words were slurred or normal but she feared the worst by the way Douglas was looking at her. "We were just out for a walk and—" She couldn't hold it in, and poor Rafael standing next to her could do nothing but follow her over to the side of the path, holding her hair again. Even in her state, Jemma felt she knew Rafael well enough to know that he wouldn't lie to Douglas. She could hear him talking in a low voice to him.

"Is she okay?" Douglas sounded worried.

"She will be. Yes. She's been sick several times in the last forty minutes, so I'm guessing she's close to the end of that. I'll try to keep her up a little while, though, to be sure that she won't be sick in her sleep."

"Shall I send Gigi over?"

"I think I can get her situated."

Jemma heard him pause.

"If that's okay with you?"

"Yes. Yes, of course. You're a fine young man, Rafael. Thanks for looking out for her. We're going to want to talk about this—but that can wait until tomorrow."

Jemma tried to stand up and keep her balance as they all three started walking down the path.

"Douglas?"

"Yes."

"I'm sorry. Please don't hate me."

Douglas stopped walking and Rafael and Jemma stopped too.

He stepped closer to her, putting his hand on her shoulder. "Honey, I could never hate you. Gigi and I love you. You know that. You go get some sleep and we'll talk about this in the morning."

She tried to smile at him but even her face hurt now.

She let Rafael lead her into the house and then down the hall to her bedroom. She watched him pull a long shirt out of her top drawer before he walked over to where she'd flopped down on the bed.

He gently took her shoes off, and she noticed that she'd practically destroyed a pair of her favorite heels. He pulled her to her feet and led her to the bathroom.

"I figure you might want to brush your teeth." He winked at her as he found her toothbrush and got it ready for her. "Can you do this, go to the bathroom and put your shirt on while I go get you some water?" He was looking at her so carefully.

She nodded, feeling only slightly confident that she could actually do the list of tasks he'd just handed out to her.

She managed to finish up in the bathroom and get herself undressed. She smiled when she saw the shirt that he'd grabbed out of her drawer. It was actually one of Dex's. Somehow she got out of her dress, into the shirt, and under the covers before she heard a quiet knock on her door that was slightly open.

"Come in." *Lovely Rafael.* She could hardly keep her eyes open and the bed felt so nice.

Rafael came over by her bed. Seemingly satisfied that she was clothed under the covers he carefully sat on the side of her bed and helped her to sit up a bit. "Here, Jemma. Drink some of this water, okay? And I brought you something for the headache you'll probably have tomorrow. Take them now. I think it will help."

She took the pills and gulped down the water, not realizing the extent of her thirst until that minute. She handed the glass back to him and he placed it on her night table.

"Do you feel better now? Your stomach, I mean?"

She nodded her head, wanting sleep, but seeing Rafael sitting next to her on the bed was stirring something else in her. She didn't know if it was the alcohol or her heart but she had the alcohol to use as an excuse anyway. She reached out her hands to wrap them around his neck, just barely grazing his lips with her own before he quickly pulled away.

"Jemma." He looked pained as he said her name, taking her hands in his as he placed them down at her side over the covers.

"What? Don't you like me?" She knew it wasn't fair. She knew that he liked her.

He was staring at her intently now and then his arms reached to tuck the covers in around her just a bit, his hand smoothing the hair away from her face. He looked at her for one more moment and as her eyes closed she felt his lips gentle on her forehead.

"Good night, Jemma."

The clock ticking in the kitchen was making her head hurt—that was how bad her hangover was—and Jemma had now sworn tequila off for good. Never again.

Rafael had come by that morning, bringing her coffee and toast before he'd told her that he was headed over to talk to Douglas. He'd wanted her to know before he had the conversation with him that he felt obligated to tell him what had happened the night before—that he wouldn't lie to him.

Jemma respected Rafael for it, only asking that he not tell them the whole story about how he'd found her with

Eduardo. She thought that it might cause them too much worry and she didn't want to do that to them. Rafael had agreed as long as he didn't have to lie outright to any questions that they had for him, which had suited Jemma.

Now she sat in the big chair in the living room across from where Gigi and Douglas were sitting together on the sofa. She had a blanket wrapped around her but she still felt cold as she tugged it closer. The look on Gigi's face pained her. She knew that she'd disappointed her, and after all her bravado in sneaking out and feeling like she needed to do her own thing, she was regretting it now.

Gigi was clearing her throat and Jemma noticed the look that passed between her and Douglas. Jemma wasn't at all sure what was going to happen, but she'd been preparing herself mentally for the worst. She'd messed up. Bad.

"So, my darling. What do you have to say for yourself?"

Gigi didn't look angry as much as she looked sad when she spoke.

Jemma looked down at her lap before she looked back up to meet Gigi's eyes. "I'm really sorry. I know I messed up."

"I just—I don't think you realize all the bad stuff that could happen to you—and that worries me, Jemma."

Jemma felt that she'd had a wake-up call of sorts last night but she wasn't going to share all of that with Gigi. It would upset her too much, and Jemma didn't want her mom to know either. She'd never been in that position before with a guy. In her heart she knew that if Rafael hadn't have shown up, things would have ended very differently the night before. Her heart pounded even thinking about it now.

"I know. You're right." Jemma looked over at Gigi and Douglas, begging them with her eyes to believe how sorry she was. "I don't know what I was thinking. It won't happen again. I promise."

She really didn't know if they'd believe her or not. Why should they really?

Gigi looked at Douglas and he nodded at her to continue.

"Douglas and I have been talking all morning—trying to figure out the best way to handle all of this. And we've not called your mother—called Blu yet, but we do intend to let her know what happened."

Jemma nodded. She understood that.

"We're not going to sugarcoat this, Jemma." Douglas was speaking now. "After seeing you last night, I was prepared to put you on the next plane to California—not because we don't want you here, but because we want you to be okay and if that means getting you into a program—then that's what it has to mean."

Rehab. She had no one to blame but herself. At least now she only had two weeks to go before her birthday— that was something, she guessed. But she couldn't stop the tears from coming as she thought about it.

"Come here, honey." Gigi was motioning for Douglas to slide over on the sofa to make room for Jemma between them. Jemma obeyed and fell into Gigi's embrace, letting her hold her for a few minutes while she cried.

"Honey, sit up and look at me for a minute."

Jemma wiped the tears away with her hand while she tried to get it together.

"I—we'd like to give you one more chance—if staying here is what you want," Gigi said, and she seemed to be studying Jemma's face carefully.

She probably doesn't know if she can trust me. Why does she trust me? Jemma nodded her head.

"But honey, a lot of things need to change around here. We need to see you being involved—not sitting in your room by yourself all day and night. We want your help around the orphanage and we also want your word that you won't have any communication with that guy."

Jemma was nodding her head again, shocked that she was being given another chance. She hugged Gigi and then Douglas.

"You can thank Gigi for this, Jemma. Honestly, it's against my better judgment but I trust that she's making the right call about this. I want to know that we can trust you to keep your word to us."

"You can. I promise. I'll start helping out more. I know I've been a brat this past week." She looked down at her lap, feeling ashamed all of a sudden. "I really am sorry."

Gigi hugged her again and then got up from the sofa. "Let's just move on from here. Douglas and I are willing to put this all behind us and move forward, if you are too, Jemma—and I mean that." Gigi had that intense look about her again. "The bottom line is that we care about you so much—we love you as if you're our own granddaughter. You know that. We can't just stand by and let your life become anything less than amazing." Gigi leaned over and kissed her on the top of the head. "You're too talented and smart to let that happen and I won't have it, so let's figure out how to get you back on track, young lady." She winked and Jemma laughed.

"I love you guys too." Jemma gave them her widest smile.

"Okay, then. You take the day—to sit in your room and do whatever—nurse that headache I bet you have, but tomorrow be ready to work."

Jemma nodded.

"I have an idea that I'm thinking of—I just need to check a few things and then we can talk about it tomorrow."

Jemma watched them walk away and then went to her room, thankful that things had gone much better than she'd expected.

CHAPTER 24

Jemma sat in the dining area eating lunch and listening to Maria chat across from her at the table. Out of the corner of her eye, she'd seen Rafael and a few of the older kids carrying big boxes and bags from the dock to one of the smaller buildings where some of the classes were held. She could hear Gigi in the distance, directing them as they made several trips back and forth.

Gigi had stopped by the dining hall earlier to check in with her and see how the day had been going so far. Jemma had made it to breakfast to help with the kids and she'd spent all morning with the toddlers and a few of the volunteers. She liked helping with the children. It reminded her of when Kylie was little and she used to beg her mom and grandma to let her babysit. She'd been at least fourteen before her mom would leave her alone at the house for just a few hours with her four-year-old sister—and Jemma had always loved every minute of it.

Instinctively, her hand went to the necklace around her neck as she thought about Kylie.

"Jemma."

"Huh? Sorry, what were you saying?"

"Earth to Jemma." Maria giggled.

"Yeah, yeah." Jemma smiled at the little girl.

"I was just asking you about the necklace. You're always playing with it. Can I see it?"

Jemma held it just out from her neck so that Maria could see the larger bead in the center.

"My sister, my best friend," Maria read out loud. "Who's that from?"

"My sister." Jemma winked at her. "Who's the same age as you, I think."

"Is she seven?"

"She is—seven and a half, actually."

"Like me." Maria smiled. "What's your sister's name?"

"Kylie."

"I like that name. It's nice."

Jemma studied her for a few seconds, noticing that her expression had changed and the little girl seemed thoughtful.

"Maria's a nice name too—a great name, in fact."

"Do you think so?" Maria's face brightened just a bit, but not enough to convince Jemma that something wasn't wrong.

"I do. What's wrong? You look a little bit sad."

Maria was looking down at her plate and when she looked up Jemma saw the tears gathered in the little girl's eyes.

She doesn't want me to see her cry. She's tough—too tough for such a young girl.

And Jemma's heart ached for her, in that moment recognizing that Maria's life hadn't always been good—that like so many of the kids from the orphanage, she might have known tough times and possibly held on to the bad memories that children shouldn't have to deal with. Jemma wanted the little girl to trust her. It seemed important.

"Come over here by me, Maria."

Maria obeyed, getting up to walk around the table, and came to sit next to her on the bench. Jemma took her hand and looked her in the eye. "You can tell me."

Maria looked up at her, wiping the few tears that had fallen with one swipe of her free hand. "I wish I had a sister."

Jemma felt a lump form in her throat. There were so many people who loved the little girl—in Jemma's eyes, Maria had lots of sisters—and brothers—and a whole family here at the orphanage. Even as she had the thought, she recognized a certain truth which she wouldn't let herself think about just yet as her focus remained on the young girl.

"Hey, wait a minute. I heard that you are going to have two sisters—*and* a brother." Jemma smiled at her.

"Yeah, but I wish I had a *real* sister—who looks like me, I mean."

"Maria."

The little girl looked up at her.

"Your parents—the ones who are adopting you— they're gonna be your real parents, you know. And those kids—your two sisters and a brother—they're gonna be your real family." Jemma smiled at the young girl. "Families look all sorts of different ways."

The words echoed in her head and she had to fight to hold back her own unexpected emotion.

Maria looked up at her with wide eyes—eyes that needed to understand—to believe what Jemma was saying to her.

"Your parents are choosing you, Maria—that's pretty special, if you ask me."

Blu had chosen to be a mother to her.

Maria suddenly turned on the bench, throwing her arms around Jemma, nearly knocking her over. "I'm gonna miss you, Jemma."

Jemma hugged her back. "I'm gonna miss you too, sweetie."

She felt guilty because she'd wasted so much time since she'd arrived there—time that she could have— should have—been spending with Maria and the other kids. Now she only had a few days left to spend with her before Maria's adoptive parents would arrive to take her back to the U.S. with them.

Jemma stood up from the bench. "Do you want to go for a walk with me?"

"Sure." Maria smiled and took Jemma's hand.

Jemma sat across from Rafael at the small dining table in their shared kitchen. She'd had a nap after her walk with Maria and woken up to a cup of tea that Rafael had made her. She eyed him carefully now, grinning because she couldn't get over how mischievous he looked. All day he'd been busy helping out with some type of big delivery that had arrived from the city, and now when she tried to press him about what it was, he was acting all funny and secretive about it.

"Okay, Raf—be that way. I'm sure Gigi will tell me what the heck the big secret is." She laughed.

"I'm sure she will."

She sipped her tea, thinking about the elephant in the room. They hadn't really seen much of one another since everything had gone down the other night and she knew that she needed to say some things to Rafael—some serious things. She felt embarrassed to bring it up, but he deserved to know how grateful she was to him.

"Rafael."

"Yeah."

"About the other night." He was looking at her so intently. "I just want you to know how much I appreciate everything you did for me." She felt a heat in her cheeks. She had a vague memory of most of the night—her being sick, but also the kiss she'd tried to get from him—a kiss that he'd not returned.

"I'm just glad that I got there in time."

"Me too. And I'm sorry—I'm sorry if I made you uncomfortable." She looked away for a second, unable to meet his eyes. "At the end of the night, I mean."

"You mean with the kiss?" He didn't look away. Jemma appreciated his boldness and she was slightly surprised by it.

She looked down again, knowing that her unwillingness to look at him gave away the fact that she was more embarrassed than he was—and rightly so. It was she that had made a spectacle of herself. "Yeah."

"Jemma, you know that it wasn't that I didn't want to kiss you, right? I've thought about kissing you ever since you arrived here last week."

"You have?"

"I have."

She wondered if he would kiss her now. She wanted him to kiss her now, but he didn't make a move to get up from the table and she wouldn't be the first to suggest it.

"I just know that you have a lot on your mind—a lot to figure out. And—well, it certainly wasn't right the other night. I'd never take advantage of you like that. I care about you too much."

There was the intense look again.

"Probably too much." His voice was quiet.

"What do you mean?" Her voice was just as quiet and her heart was beating fast in her chest as she waited for him to answer.

"I just want you to figure out what it is you need—for you, I mean. And I just—I think that it will probably mean you'll be leaving soon."

Jemma was nodding. He was right. She would be leaving.

"And?"

"And mostly I care about our friendship. I'd like for us to be better friends, actually. And I don't want to do anything to ruin that. Does that make sense?"

She was nodding her head slowly, the words that Chase had spoken to her so many times playing back in her mind—about finding a guy that cherished and respected her. Heck, she hadn't even really known what that meant—until Rafael. She'd never known a guy like Rafael. Any woman would be lucky to have him for a boyfriend. And she was just as lucky to have him for a friend. She really understood that now.

Rafael got up from the table just as Gigi entered the house, a wide grin on her face as she made her way to the kitchen. Jemma got up too, making her way around the table to give Rafael a big hug.

"Thank you." She pulled back to look him in the eyes. "You're a great friend, Rafael."

"Am I interrupting something here?" Gigi said once Jemma had pulled back from Rafael.

"No, I was just heading to my room," said Rafael.

Jemma was certain that she saw a look pass between him and Gigi, and once again she felt as though she was on the outside of a secret. She gave Gigi a big hug when she walked over to where Jemma was standing.

"Will you come with me? I want to show you something before dinner."

"Gigi, what is it? I feel like there's something going on around here that everyone knows about except me."

"Oh, who's everyone?" Gigi was teasing her and Jemma was thankful that nothing felt awkward between them.

"Oh, I dunno. Just Rafael, all the boxes and now you." Jemma laughed. "Okay, I'm ready anytime you are."

Gigi took her by the hand and they headed out the door.

CHAPTER 25

Jemma stood in the center of the room, looking around her in amazement. It was the art studio that she'd dreamed of as a child. It was the very same studio that she remembered sketching on a big piece of paper with Gigi when she'd been there the summer that she was fifteen. She'd been trying to tell Gigi that they needed it at the orphanage—a place where the kids could create. And now she was standing in the center of the most beautiful room.

Large easels were set up in a semicircle around the room and there were shelf upon shelf of every art supply one could possibly need. Light was streaming in from the big windows and her favorite rock music was playing from a stereo in the corner. Hearing the music reminded her of her mother. Jemma's taste in rock music was more modern than what Blu called the classics but they both loved to crank it up when they were really trying to focus on something.

Jemma walked over to one of the easels, running her

fingers over the large blank piece of paper.

"I talked to a woman I know in the city who runs an art supply store. She assured me that you'd have everything that you need—there's also the better quality paper over in the cupboards—for when you're ready for that."

Jemma was confused as she looked around the room and then over to Gigi, who was standing there with a wide grin across her face.

"Need for what? What is all this?"

"Well…" Gigi came over to take Jemma's hands in her own. "I was hoping that you'd agree to teach the kids art—to run a class for them here."

"But Gi—"

"Don't worry. I know that you'll probably be leaving us soon and that's fine—well, it's not fine but I understand." She laughed lightly. "But we'll continue to use it and it will be here for whenever you come back. I think it will be good for the kids—to have a place where they can come to create." She winked at Jemma. "Don't you think so?"

Jemma reached out her arms to hug Gigi close. "Oh I love it. It's so beautiful. And yes—I'll be happy to work with the kids. I think that sounds fun." She was already thinking of some first projects that she might like to do with them.

"And of course, this room is yours to use as often as you like. I haven't seen you sketching or painting in such a long time, so I was hoping that you hadn't lost interest."

"You're right. It has been a long time, but you know what?"

"What, honey?"

"I think I really miss it." She couldn't wait to start painting something. "Thank you." She leaned over to kiss Gigi on the cheek.

"You're welcome."

"I mean for everything. You and Douglas have done so much for me, and I've been such a spoiled brat."

Gigi was smiling at her and laughing. "Honey, remember what I told you in the hospital?" She winked.

Jemma did remember and laughed along with her. "That I'd just lost my mind a little bit?"

"That's right. And I think you're coming around now." Gigi put her arm around her as they made their way to the door.

With a flourish Maria set the two plates of lime pie down on the table in front of Jemma and Rafael. "I had to wait until Fernanda was going to the market in town to get the limes—that's why there was a slight delay." She grinned.

"Well, that looks fantastic," Jemma said as she dug her fork into the perfect-looking dessert.

"Oh, Maria's pie is definitely worth the wait." Rafael winked as he had his first bite. "I'm gonna miss you so much."

Maria put her hands on her hips and did a fake pout with her lips. "Why, because I won't be here to make you desserts any more?"

Rafael was nodding, but then he reached out to tug on the little girl's hair playfully. "Just kidding, Maria. Seriously, it's gonna be very weird without you here."

Maria looked down for a second, and Jemma saw the tears before the girl quickly wiped them away. "I know. I'm gonna be sad too—even though I'm also excited to see my new home in America."

Jemma patted the bench beside her. "Sit down for a second. I wanna tell you something."

Maria obliged, sliding in close to Jemma to put her head against Jemma's arm. "Yes, my dear Jemma."

The gesture was so like something that Kylie would do, that Jemma burst out laughing. "You're so silly."

"I'm a regular comedian." Maria raised her eyebrows up and down.

"That you are. So I wanted you to the be the first to know that we're going to be starting an art class."

"So you've seen the studio? I was wondering when Mama Gi was going to show you. Isn't it wonderful?" Maria was grinning at her.

"So you were in on the secret?" Jemma reached over to tickle her for a second. "It is great, yes. I can't wait to start teaching in there tomorrow. Can I count on you to be one of my star pupils?"

Maria got up off the bench and did a little curtsy. "But of course. I would be honored."

Rafael and Jemma both laughed.

"And now, my friends, I must go back to work." Maria bent down to give Jemma a hug before she ran off to do her kitchen duties.

Jemma looked at Rafael as Maria ran off. "She really is quite funny, isn't she? I wonder where that comes from."

"I don't know. She's always been our little entertainer around here. I'm going to miss her."

Jemma thought Rafael looked sweet when he talked about the little girl. So many of the kids that had been at the orphanage for so long were like brothers and sisters, many of them young enough when they came that they didn't remember a life without one another.

She was going to miss Maria also, even though she didn't think she'd be at the orphanage for much longer herself. She knew now that she wanted to come back to visit. Not having Maria there when she did would be strange, but she had to be happy for the little girl who was excited about being adopted and having a family. Jemma would enjoy the next few days that they did have with her, and try to make them special for Maria.

PAULA KAY

CHAPTER 26

Everything seemed perfect to Jemma—the way the paintbrush felt in her fingers, the soft music playing in the background, the light streaming in through the windows—but the thing that felt the most perfect of all was the children standing at their easels, laughing as they made their first attempts to paint their self-portraits. Jemma was having the time of her life teaching the kids about color and the various ways that they could use the paintbrush or charcoal to express themselves.

She stood behind Maria while she worked, taking careful strokes with her brush and somehow creating something beyond what Jemma would have thought possible for a beginner. She leaned down to whisper close to Maria's ear. "You are very talented. Remember that, okay?" Maria turned around to look at her with wide eyes. Jemma nodded.

She continued to make her way around the room. The children were there by choice. Gigi had announced to the older kids that the art class was now an option for them during what would normally be a study period. So far Jemma's class consisted of eight girls and four boys.

She also had the toddlers coming in during the day to do art projects with her and one of the other volunteers. She loved getting messy with the two- and three-year-olds as they finger-painted and made their own masterpieces to hang up in the dining hall where everyone could admire them.

She walked back over to her easel in the corner of the room to work on her own self-portrait. She bit her bottom lip as she looked at what she'd done. It was almost complete, and there was something about it that wasn't quite right.

Out of the corner of her eye, she noticed Rafael in the doorway, leaning against the frame, smiling; he seemed to be taking in the room before he made his way over to Jemma.

"That looks amazing."

Jemma smiled at him. "Do you think so? I feel like there's something missing."

Rafael studied the painting for several seconds. "It's the light…"

"What do you mean?"

"It doesn't have the light in your eyes—they look sort of flat, unhappy."

Jemma winked at him. "I guess I must be painting a self-portrait of me when I first arrived, then."

Rafael gave Jemma a slight hug and looked her in the eye. "Well, I don't think that's who you are now."

Jemma followed his eyes as he looked at the children around the room, all of them deep in concentration of their paintings, with big smiles on their faces. She felt the broad grin on her own face and she knew that he was right.

"You're right. I need a few more minutes, and I think this painting will be done."

Rafael had a funny look on his face.

"What, Raf?"

"What are you going to do with it? The self-portrait?"

"I dunno. I was thinking of giving it to Gigi."

"Oh."

Jemma felt a lump in her throat. "You can have it if you want it."

"Thank you. I'd like that."

Jemma smiled and reached over to give Rafael a quick kiss on the cheek.

CHAPTER 27

It had been an eventful day. The party for Maria was a fitting ending to introduce her new family to everyone at Casa de los Niños and also a great way to let the children say goodbye to someone who had been a big part of their family there.

Jemma had been nearby when the Millers had arrived and they and Maria saw one another for the first time. Maria had been shy at first, but the tears and hugs that came quickly from Mr. and Mrs. Miller seemed to relax the little girl right away.

Soon after, Maria had run off with her new siblings to show them around the orphanage, and Jemma had been able to witness the breakdown that Mrs. Miller had with her husband from afar. She'd been overcome with joy and the realization that Maria was going to be their daughter. The whole scene had brought unexpected tears to Jemma's eyes, and she'd felt privileged to witness it.

Now, at the party, Jemma watched Gigi and Douglas from across the room. Douglas's arm was around Gigi and she was wiping tears from her eyes as they watched

Maria with her new family. Jemma crossed the room to where they stood.

"Are you two okay?" She smiled at them, her own heart tugging as she thought about Maria not being there the next day.

"Yes." Gigi returned the smile. "It's hard to see her go and it doesn't happen much around here—that the kids get adopted—but Maria's going to have a good life with the Millers. I'm sure of that." She looked at Douglas, who was nodding his head in agreement.

"Yes, they're good people. She'll be happy there," he agreed.

Jemma was thoughtful.

"What is it, honey?" Gigi put her arm around her.

"Oh, I've just been thinking so much lately—about families."

"They look all sorts of different ways, don't they?" Douglas winked at her. "Gigi and I never could have conceived that our family could grow so big, but now I can't imagine it any other way."

Gigi laughed. "That's for sure."

Jemma watched Maria, playing and laughing with her new sisters and brothers across the room—her new family that was going to take her in and love her as if she was born to belong with them. She looked at Gigi and Douglas, who would also continue to love the child from afar, and she doubted that Maria would forget the years of love that they'd poured into her life at the orphanage.

"I think it's time I make a phone call—to my mother." Jemma said as she wiped a tear from her eye. "Douglas, can I use your office?"

"Of course." He winked at her.

Gigi grinned and gave her a big hug. "I love you, darling girl. You go do what you need to do."

Jemma grinned back at both of them. "Thank you."

Jemma was a little nervous as she waited for her mom to answer on the other end of the line. She'd been taking to her once in awhile, but her stubbornness had gotten in the way of any real conversation. This call—initiated by her—was going to be different.

It was time for forgiveness. Jemma knew that now. The only way that she was going to be able to move forward in her own life was going to be to forgive her mom and grandmother and let the past stay in the past, accepting the fact that they both loved her and always would.

"Hello."

"Mom?"

"Jemma—honey, how are you?"

Jemma could imagine her mom's wide grin and she suddenly ached with missing her.

"Mom." And just like that she burst into tears.

"Honey. What is it? Are you okay?" Her mother waited while Jemma tried to stop crying enough to get the words out. "Jemma, you're scaring me a little bit. Are Gigi and Douglas okay?" Her voice went quieter as she asked the question.

"Yes. Everyone's fine." Jemma took a deep breath. "I just—I just needed to talk to you. Is Grandma there too?"

"She is, yes. Do you want me to go get her?"

"Yes, would you—and then put your phone on speaker so that I can talk to both of you."

She waited a few minutes—just long enough to collect her words again—for her mom to come back to the phone.

"Okay, we're both here now."

"Hi, Jemma. We miss you around here." It was her grandma's voice in her ear.

It had all been so wonderful—when her grandmother had come into Jemma's life after so many years of not knowing her or even that she'd existed. Jemma now realized that she didn't have to let her initial shock and confusion about the truth destroy the relationships that she had with either her mom or her grandmother.

She—and they—could decide how their family would look and the truth was that Blu *had* been the only mother Jemma had ever known. And she'd been a great mother to her. Jemma knew now that she didn't want anything to change in their relationship—well, apart from the fact that *she* needed to change—to be a better daughter.

"Hi, Grandma." Jemma smiled, missing them both.

Everyone was quiet for a few moments. Jemma could

guess that they were wondering what it was that she had to tell them, and she wouldn't prolong it anymore.

"I just really wanted to tell you both how much I love you." She was crying now, but the tears felt so good—so real to her. She didn't try to stop them.

"I love you too, honey." It was her mom.

"We both love you so much." Her grandmother sounded like she was crying too.

"Honey, I know I messed up—on keeping the truth from you for so long—but I just—I didn't know how to tell you. I didn't want anything to change the fact that you've been my daughter for all these years. That's the truth, Jemma—no matter what, that will always be the truth."

Jemma had thought a lot about it over the past few days. She'd thought about her conversations with Maria and her relationship with her own sister Kylie—or more accurately Kylie, not actually her sister by blood at all— but it didn't change anything for Jemma. She would always be Kylie's big sister; and she knew in her heart that if she could imagine a circumstance like the one her mom had gone through when Jemma had been born—if that would have been her and Kylie—she would have made the same choices. She knew that now. It wasn't hard to imagine.

"I know." Jemma brought her attention back to the phone call and the two women in her life who loved her most of all. "And I know that you will always be my mother—and that you've always been there for me. And I've been such a brat lately. I know that now."

Her mom was laughing lightly on the other end. "Well, you've been a teen-ager—that's for sure."

Jemma smiled. She'd been more than just a teen-ager. She'd put them all through way too much lately.

"And Grandma?"

"Yes. I'm here."

"I'm just so thankful that you did come back into our lives—that everything had worked out the way that it had. I'll admit that it's all still strange when I think about it, but I think it will just take some time, ya know? But I'm not angry anymore. I only want to move forward."

"Me too." Her grandmother sounded like she was crying now as well.

"Jemma, you sound so grown-up all of a sudden." Blu was laughing as she made the statement.

Jemma laughed also. "Well, I am about to turn eighteen, you know."

"Yes, I do know. And I wish that you were here so that we could celebrate with you, honey."

Jemma suddenly wished that too. She missed them. She missed her home. But she also knew that it was nearing the time that she'd say goodbye for just awhile. But for all the right reasons—not because she'd gone and lost her mind just a little bit. She smiled, remembering Gigi's words that had made her laugh during one of the hardest times in her life.

She was starting to have an idea about what she wanted. She wasn't ready to talk about it just yet but it was the first time in a long while that she'd felt true excitement for her future—for everything that was ahead for her—everything that Arianna had ever imagined for the little girl she'd called J-bean. Jemma smiled as she thought about Arianna and how much she'd love her.

"Jemma? Are you still there?" Her mother was asking.

"Sorry. Just a lot of thoughts going on in my head—all good, exciting thoughts."

"I can't wait to hear about that," said Blu.

"Me too," said Linda.

"Well, I will call you again in a few days. I promise. I should go now. We're having a party here, but I needed to slip away to call you—to tell you both that I love you very much and I'm very sorry for everything I've put you through."

"I'm the one that's sorry, Jemma. And I love you too—very much," said Blu.

"As do I, lovely girl. I can't wait to see you soon," said her grandmother.

"Mom, will you please tell Chase that I'm sorry too—and thank him for not killing me." Jemma laughed. "And tell him that I love him." She got a lump in her throat when she thought about how much Chase had been there for her—being the perfect father figure, yet never pushing her to accept him as such. But he'd been steadfast and steady in his role as someone she knew would always be looking out for her.

"I will. Sure."

"And give Kylie the biggest squeeze for me. Tell her I'll call her soon. I love you."

Jemma got off the phone and wiped her eyes with her sleeve. She felt different. She felt older—like she was coming into the women she was meant to be.

CHAPTER 28

Jemma was sitting in the small living room area that she shared with Rafael. They were having a cup of tea and she'd brought her laptop out to check her e-mail. She loved the easy friendship that had been developing between her and Rafael over the past week. He'd been right about the fact that pursuing anything else—at least for right now—would have been a mistake. Jemma knew that now, because Rafael was turning out to be one of the best friends she'd ever had—certainly one of her best guy friends.

Over the past few days they'd spent hours talking—their nightly chats running well into the early hours of the morning. They were both at a crossroads—Jemma about to turn eighteen and everything that meant for her regarding the vast amount of money she was about to have access to—and Rafael with his own dream for a future that he'd finally shared with her. Rafael wanted to move to the city and start his own construction business.

Tonight they were enjoying an easy silence—Rafael

reading a book and Jemma on her computer.

"Wow." Jemma was in shock and didn't even realize she'd spoken out loud.

"What is it?" Rafael looked up from his book.

Jemma didn't even have time to think if it was a good idea to share the latest with Rafael—she was too surprised to second-guess her reaction.

"It's Dex."

A few nights ago, she'd finally told Rafael everything about Dex and their history together. She'd not held anything back and neither had he as he expressed his disdain for the guy who'd once claimed to love Jemma.

"What, Jemma? What's going on?"

Jemma saw the concern on Rafael's face and regretted that she'd brought it up without processing everything herself first. How did she feel? She wasn't sure at all, but getting his e-mail had made her heart beat faster for a few seconds.

Fire. She'd be playing with fire. Entertaining any thoughts of Dex was a dangerous game—one she shouldn't want anything to do with.

She turned her attention back to the e-mail and Rafael's question.

"I just got an e-mail from him."

"And?"

"And he's back in San Diego. He didn't say, but I'm guessing that means that things between him and his new LA girlfriend hadn't worked out."

Rafael rolled his eyes. "Shocking."

Jemma had told him about Andrea and all the people they'd been living with—and partying with—in LA. Rafael had said that the idea of Jemma living in that environment seemed foreign to him—that even though he had seen her drunk and out of it since she'd been at the orphanage, he knew that it wasn't who she really was—that she was much better than all that.

Jemma looked at Rafael carefully, debating if she should say more. "He says he wants me back—that I should come home to live with him and his brother."

Am I even entertaining the idea?

"Jemma." Rafael looked pained as he said her name. "No. You can't even be considering that." He reached over to put his hand on her arm and she didn't pull away. "You're not, are you?"

She shook her head slowly. *Am I?* "No. Not really."

She knew Rafael was right—that she should be adamant about staying far away from Dex, but there was something about him—about her past with him.

It's just a habit—he's just a habit.

Her thoughts were much clearer lately. Gigi had been right about the good that it would do Jemma in coming to the orphanage. It *had* been the case that she'd had time to think about things—what she wanted in her life—here at the orphanage. At least it had once she'd stopped being such an idiot and given herself time to really think and feel. Ideas had been coming and she was close to putting together some next steps to making those dreams of hers a reality. Would she really discard all of that after one e-mail from Dex?

She shook her head as if doing so could brush away the disturbing thoughts from her mind. She closed her computer and stood up from where she'd been sitting next to Rafael, noticing his eyes on her the whole time. She needed to clear her head—to sleep on everything, trusting that she'd be able to make the right decisions when it came to Dex or anything in her life from now on.

She had to start trusting herself, and there was no reason not to. She'd learned that much from her experiences over the past two weeks—the good and the bad. She knew that she needed to grow up and stop hiding away from things—and she had been doing that. She just needed to keep reminding herself.

Rafael got up from his chair and gave Jemma a hug.

She loved how open he was with his emotions. It was a quality that she'd not seen in many guys—certainly not in any of the guys that she'd been hanging out with. She trusted Rafael and she didn't want to disappoint him. She didn't want him to look at her in any other way than how she'd ever seen him look at her—which was a look of respect. And it was funny because it seemed to make her respect herself that much more.

He'd taken a step back now to look her in the eyes. "Just think long and hard about things, okay?"

She nodded. "I will." He looked so concerned. "I

promise, Raf."

"I know you will. Sleep well."

Jemma crawled into bed that night with thoughts of Dex and her new dreams all jumbled together—somehow her brain wanted to find a way to make it all work—to find the possibility that maybe Dex could fit into her new life—her new dreams for a future. Maybe Dex had changed too? But as she drifted off to sleep, she knew that Dex hadn't changed—that to go back to Dex would be to go back to her old life and a person that she didn't want to be any more.

CHAPTER 29

The morning in the studio was quiet—just the way she liked it. Jemma had been getting up earlier and earlier the last few days to work on a project that she'd started the day after she and her mom had had their big talk. She turned her music on—keeping the volume low this morning. She had so much on her mind, and somehow she knew that this morning's painting session was sure to help her think clearly. She walked over to the easel in the corner of the room and uncovered her work in progress. She'd been surprised at how easy it had been to get back into her painting.

And she loved to paint. How could she have forgotten? Blu had gotten her private lessons with a local artist in San Diego one summer, and the hours Jemma had spent with her in her beach studio had been pivotal to her work. Her family had always been supportive of her art and thought she was amazing, but she'd always doubted whether or not she had real talent—back then, she just knew that it was something that she loved to do, something that relaxed her.

But her time with the artist had been special. She'd told Jemma that she had real talent—that she was very special and should always pursue her art no matter what. Jemma sighed as she remembered that summer and those words that had meant everything to her. She really had gone on to lose her mind a little bit—more than a little bit, as she'd almost thrown away all of her dreams—and for what? For nothing, really—a life of partying and being with the wrong guy who could never really love her and plan a future with her.

Jemma bit her bottom lip as she studied the photo pinned to the top of her easel.

She heard a sharp intake of breath from behind her.

"Oh, it's gorgeous." It was Gigi, and she was staring at the portrait that Jemma had been working on.

Jemma had been so engrossed in her thoughts and the image that she'd not heard Gigi come in. She turned toward her now to see the tears in her eyes, the smile wide on her face.

"Do you think so?"

Gigi was nodding and wiping away a tear.

"It's for my Mom. I thought she might like to hang it in her studio."

Jemma had found the photo in the small stack of the ones she'd grabbed from her bedside table back at the beach house—right before she ran away to LA. It was a picture taken out on their deck of Blu, Jemma, and Arianna. It was one of the best memories Jemma had of

Arianna—the weekend that she'd taken them to the beach house for the first time.

"I brought us some coffee."

Jemma saw the two mugs sitting on the small table in the corner of the studio. She nodded her head and then unpinned the photo to bring it over to the table with her.

"So you're up very early these days." Gigi laughed lightly.

"I know. Can you believe it?" Jemma laughed too. "I guess I have a lot on my mind. And I'm also really enjoying the studio. I can't thank you enough for everything. I feel so different from that silly girl who arrived here just a few short weeks ago."

Gigi reached out to put her hand on Jemma's arm. "Well, you look like a totally different girl. Still just as beautiful but much happier and—oh, I don't know—a little wiser maybe?" Gigi winked at her.

"Well, let's hope so." Jemma laughed, the e-mail from Dex still fresh on her mind. "Speaking of…"

"Uh-oh. What's that look I'm seeing?"

Jemma knew she was going to tell Gigi. There was no point of holding anything back any more—not if she truly wanted to start making better choices and move her life forward in the way that was best for her.

"Well. I got an e-mail from Dex." She heard Gigi's intake of breath.

"And?"

"And he wants me to come be with him. He's back in

San Diego now."

Gigi was eyeing her and Jemma could imagine the thoughts swirling in her head—she was really so good at being careful with Jemma—it was how she'd always handled her.

"You don't have to worry." Jemma smiled and it was her turn to reach out and take Gigi's hand. "I'd be crazy to go back to that—to Dex and that lifestyle. It's not what I want—not any more."

"Good. You have no idea what a relief your words are to me." Gigi laughed, reaching for the photo on the table. "May I?"

Jemma nodded and Gigi picked it up to study it more closely.

"Tell me about Ari," Jemma said. Gigi looked at her and smiled. "I mean, I do have some great memories, but I wish I could remember more—I wish I'd known her when I was older."

"Ari would have loved to know you now—the young woman you've become."

"It's pretty amazing—what she did for my mom—the beach house and everything. And what she did for me—do you know why she did it? Why she left me all the money?"

"Ari loved your mom and you very much. From the moment she met her, she and your mom were almost inseparable."

"And when she met me?" Jemma had heard the story

many times. About how surprised Arianna had been to find out that Blu had a daughter. Jemma had been three at the time—the same age as the daughter that Arianna had given up for adoption.

"Well, when she met you, she was all set to not be won over—it was painful for her to imagine her own daughter the same age, as you can imagine."

"But my cuteness was too irresistible." Jemma laughed.

"Well, yes. That's the truth. You were very cute and irresistible. That was for sure." Gigi laughed too, enjoying the memories that didn't make her feel quite as sad as they once did. "You won us all over, actually."

Jemma smiled, and she reached for the photo that Gigi had placed back on the table.

"What do you think Ari thought I would do when I got older? With the money, I mean?"

Gigi looked thoughtful. "We talked about you— during those last days of Ari's life. She didn't tell me everything—about your trust or all of her plans for each of us. But I know that she wanted you to be happy. She talked about your dancing and how she wanted to be sure that you'd be able to continue with your classes—for as long as you enjoyed it. Ari had made that pretty clear."

"So she really didn't expect me to use some of the money for college, then? Mom always told me that the money was for me to do with as I liked but that she hoped I'd use some of it for my education. Well, then I got a little crazy, so I'm sure you all have been worried about what I'd actually be doing with all that money." Jemma laughed and Gigi put on a stern face.

"Well, ain't that the truth." She eyed Jemma carefully. "Honestly, when things were pretty bad, we'd all been talking to Douglas—to see if there was anything that could be done about keeping the money from you a little longer—just until you'd come to your senses." She winked at Jemma.

"But now my birthday is almost here—and I know that there wasn't anything to be done differently. Douglas already told me that." Jemma laughed. "And it's a good thing I have come to my senses then, huh?"

"You can say that again."

The two women sat in silence for a few seconds, sipping their coffee, the photo in the center of the table again.

"Gigi. I think I know what I want to do."

CHAPTER 30

Gigi had been very excited and totally on board when Jemma had shared with her that she wanted to go to Italy—to study art and to paint. That was her future; she'd known it from the moment Gigi had shown her the art studio just a short week ago.

Once she'd shared her idea with Gigi, the wheels were in motion. Gigi had fired off an e-mail to Lia and soon after, Jemma was talking to Lia on the phone, accepting an invitation to come stay with them at the vineyard for as long as she liked—she'd said that Gabriela loved the idea and now couldn't stop talking about it.

This news had made Jemma smile. Lia and Antonio had adopted Gabriela from Casa de los Niños six years ago when she'd been only one, and she'd been a perfect fit for the whole extended family.

Jemma was getting more excited every day and by the time Gigi had finally told her that they'd all be going to Italy with her—she, Douglas, and Jemma's whole family—to see her off on this next adventure in her life,

Jemma could hardly contain her excitement.

It had been long enough that she'd been apart from her family. She was ready to see them all. She and Gigi would meet them in San Diego and then they'd head to Italy. Douglas would meet them a few days later once Tori and the other volunteers were all set to take over from him at the orphanage.

Everything was coming together and now she was having the best birthday of her life, celebrating at the party that the children had put together for her.

"Well, that sure looks like the smile of one happy birthday girl."

Rafael came up to her, pulling her in for a big hug.

Jemma felt herself grinning, the way she always did when Rafael was nearby, always so complimentary and positive.

He stood back from her with that intense stare he often had.

"What?" Jemma laughed, swiping her hand across her mouth at imaginary crumbs. "Is there something on my face."

"It's just—it's nice to see you looking so happy." He was smiling at her.

She returned the smile. "I am happy—happier than I've been in a long time."

"Good. You deserve it. And happy birthday." He grew somber. "I'm really gonna miss you, Jemma."

Jemma reached out to take his hand. "I'm going to

miss you too, Rafael. A lot. Thank goodness for technology these days—you have to promise me that you're going to keep in touch."

Rafael was nodding his head as Jemma pulled him out of the way to a quieter place in the open space where the kids were dancing and having a good time.

"I want to tell you something."

Jemma was a little nervous and she wasn't sure why exactly.

Rafael looked slightly nervous too, and she could tell by the look on his face that he wasn't at all sure about what Jemma was about to tell him.

Jemma laughed to lighten the mood. "It's nothing bad." She smiled at him. It wasn't bad at all. If only he would take her up on her offer.

"Okay. Are you going to make me guess?" He winked.

"No. No guessing necessary. I'd like to offer you a business proposition."

Rafael looked confused.

"For the construction company you want to start."

She saw Rafael's face soften and the light come into his eyes as it often did when he talked to her about the business he wanted to start.

"Okay. Go on."

"I've talked to Douglas about a few different ways that we could structure it. What I'd like to do is go into partnership with you. I'll put up the money—for whatever you need to get going, including your living costs for the move to the city—and you'll run everything. I'll be a silent partner. Don't worry." She laughed.

"Wow. Jemma, I don't know what to say."

"Or—I have one other idea—before you say anything. I could also just make you a loan, leaving me out of the business entirely. I'm good with whatever you decide." She grinned, hoping that he could feel her genuine desire to want to help him realize his own dreams as she was also moving toward hers. "I just want to help you make this happen, Raf. And it's an easy thing for me to do—now that I have the money—so you have to say yes, okay?"

She was batting her eyelashes at him—fake flirting, he'd been calling it lately.

He pulled her in for a hug. "Thank you. I don't know what to say. I really can't believe that you'd do that for me."

"Of course." She gave him a long look. "You've been a good friend to me, Rafael. I won't forget that." She wiped a tear away as they hugged again.

CHAPTER 31

Jemma had been getting up early to paint ever since they'd arrived in Tuscany a week ago. Each morning she tried to capture the colors of the sun rising beyond the vineyard. It was more beautiful than anything she'd ever seen, and she couldn't seem to get the colors in her painting just right to describe the scene in front of her. The fact that Lia and Antonio had set up an easel for her, both outside on the patio and in the spacious room they'd given her in the large villa, had meant everything to her.

The past months—years even—of her teen-age life were a blur. The past was forgotten and her future welcomed with arms wide open by those who had loved her for most of her life—all of them just as supportive of her as they'd ever been.

She shivered in the crisp morning air, pulling her sweater tighter around her, turning her head toward the sound of the door opening to the outside patio.

"Morning. I brought you something—if you can take a break."

Jemma smiled when she saw her mom putting the two coffee cups down on the patio table, a light steam coming off them and a smell that brought with it a flash of memory from her childhood—she must have been about eight at the time.

Her mom had always been so amazed when she'd find her out on the deck sketching or painting with her watercolors as the sun came up. She'd make Jemma a cup of hot chocolate, just the way she loved it—with warm milk and real whipped cream—and they'd sit out on the deck quietly together. Sometimes they'd talk, but often her mother would just sit and watch her paint while she sipped her coffee.

Jemma came over to where her mom sat now and wrapped her arms around her from behind. "You're up early too." She kissed her on the cheek before she sat down opposite her, breathing in the steam from the warm chocolate before she took a first sip. "Just the way I love it." She smiled at her mom. "Thank you."

Blu looked at her intently and Jemma thought her eyes looked teary.

"What is it? Are you okay?"

Blu was nodding her head but a few tears had made their way down her face.

"Mom? What?"

"Honey, I'm just so proud of you."

Jemma's heart stopped beating so fast as she relaxed enough to hear the words her mom was telling her.

"I was just watching you—from the window—while you were painting."

Jemma reached over to hold her mom's hand. "I know. I've come a long way. I've changed, I suppose—which is a good thing, right?" She laughed.

"You've made some wonderful decisions about your future and I see the changes that you've made since—since you found out the truth, yes. But I want you to know that I—Chase and I—never doubted you. Not really. I knew that you'd come around and I'm just so thankful that everything has turned out the way that it has."

Jemma was wiping at some tears now too. She hadn't actually known that she was going to turn out alright—not at all—not until she'd arrived at the orphanage. "I think I owe a lot to Gigi and Douglas, you know?"

"Yes, I do know." Blu squeezed her hand. "We're very lucky, aren't we?"

Jemma nodded and the two sat in comfortable silence for a few minutes before Blu's phone on the table buzzed with a notification. Blu glanced at it and went back to its home screen, grinning as she held it up so that Jemma could see it.

"I couldn't bear to leave it behind, so I took a picture of it."

It was the portrait that Jemma had painted for her mom while she was at the orphanage—of the two of them with Arianna. Douglas had had it shipped to

California and when her mom had received it, she'd called Jemma in tears. Jemma smiled now as she looked at the image on the phone. She had done a good job capturing their expressions—it had turned out exactly as she'd wanted it to.

"I can remember that day as if it were yesterday." Blu smiled as she recounted what Jemma had heard before.

*"That was the day you met Chase." Jemma interjected, grinning.

"Well, yes. But also it was just a really good day. Arianna had still been feeling well then and we'd had so much fun with you at the beach and sipping wine outside on the deck."

Jemma watched her mom's face as she looked out toward the expansive view of the vineyard.

"Ari would have loved it here—and to see you all grown up." Blu smiled at her. "She'd be just as proud of you as I am—as we all are."

"Ari's a big part of our lives—even now, I mean—isn't she?" Jemma had been thinking about Arianna a lot lately, poring over the photos that she had of her and trying to remember every detail of the memories that she did have of the times that she'd spent with her as a child.

"She is, yes." Blu reached over to take her phone from Jemma, looking at the picture again. "I'm glad that you can remember her."

"Me too," Jemma said and they finished their hot chocolate in silence, Jemma remembering the young woman who had meant so much to her—who had done so much for her—and guessing that her mom's thoughts were much the same.

CHAPTER 32

Jemma looked around the table at all the people she loved. Her family.

She watched Lia bring out the heaping plates of food—the pastas and the meat dishes that always tasted so much more delicious when they were eating them in Italy all together at the villa. Jemma loved it there. She'd forgotten how much. She and Lia had had a long walk the night before and she'd told Jemma that she was welcome to stay at the villa with them as long as she liked—that she always had a room there—and that Gabriela was beyond excited about having her there.

They were all seated now, Gabriela and Kylie laughing at one end of the table, Antonio pouring the wine. He'd said it was one of the finest from their vineyard, and after some discussion between Blu and Lia, they'd all agreed that it was fine for Jemma to be drinking one glass of wine with dinner while she was in Italy. Jemma had laughed when they'd had the discussion. Her drinking days were behind her now, but she appreciated that they were all treating her like the adult she now was.

A lot was behind her—all of the bad stuff anyway. She was determined to have the future that Arianna had imagined for her when she'd set up Jemma's trust—a future that she could be passionate about and proud of.

Antonio was standing at one end of the table, his glass raised, ready to make a toast.

"Honey, can you put your phone away?" Gigi was saying to Douglas.

Jemma glanced over toward them, laughing because it was unusual for Douglas to need to be told such a thing. He had better manners than most men Jemma knew. But now he had a very funny look on his face as he put his phone down.

"You guys aren't going to believe this."

All eyes were on him and Jemma thought he looked like he'd gone a little pale.

"What it is? Is everything alright?" Lia asked.

"I just got an e-mail." He hesitated for a moment. "From a young girl in Connecticut who says that she's Arianna's daughter."

Jemma saw the shocked look pass between Lia and Antonio, and she wasn't exactly sure why but her heart skipped a beat at the magnitude of what Douglas was telling them all in that moment. Even Gabriela and Kylie had stopped their chatter to stare intently at Douglas. He was smiling widely at Gigi, who had reached out to hold his hand beside him.

"Her name is Isabella."

ABOUT THE AUTHOR

Paula Kay spent her childhood in a small town alongside the Mississippi River in Wisconsin. (Go Packers!) As a child, she used to climb the bluffs and stare out across the mighty river—dreaming of far away lands and adventures.

Today, by some great miracle (and a lot of determination) she is able to travel, write and live in multiple locations, always grateful for the opportunity to meet new people and experience new cultures.

She enjoys Christian music, long chats with friends, reading (and writing) books that make her cry and just a tad too much reality TV.

Paula loves to hear from her readers and can be contacted via her website where you can also download a complimentary book of short stories.

PaulaKayBooks.com

ALL TITLES BY PAULA KAY

http://Amazon.com/author/paulakay

The Complete Legacy Series

Buying Time
In Her Own Time
Matter of Time
Taking Time
Just in Time
All in Good Time

Visit the author website at PaulaKayBooks.com to get on the notification list for new releases and special offers—and to also receive the complimentary download of "The Bridge: A Collection of Short Stories."

Made in the USA
Middletown, DE
11 September 2022

10196519R00137